AZURE: A JOURNAL OF LITERARY THOUGHT

a project of

Lazuli Literary Group

AZURE: A JOURNAL OF LITERARY THOUGHT
Volume Five

Edited by
Sakina B. Fakhri

with

Illustrations by
Evgenia Barsheva

LAZULI LITERARY GROUP
New York | 2022

Lazuli Literary Group is a platform dedicated to fostering the delight of the literary imagination through a small publishing press, writing contests, and an online/print literary journal, *AZURE: A Journal of Literary Thought*. We are particularly drawn to writing that broadens the concept of "literary" to one that pulls from a global pedigree of storytelling technique. We seek authors who revel in the rhythmic possibilities of the poetic line, who contemplate the flavor, the shape, and the history of every word they use; who are so committed to the pyrotechnics of the written word that they comprehend the beauty of classical forms and yet feel compelled to constantly re-invent their craft. Our goal is to support underrepresented styles of writing, specifically within a genre that we have imagined, which we call otherworld realism. We like work that generates an eclectic mix of literary, lyrical, experimental and witty reading experiences; as such, we publish works that may not be suited for mass consumption due to their raw yet polished innovations in content and form.

Published by Lazuli Literary Group | New York

www.LazuliLiteraryGroup.com

ISBN: 978-0-9994243-5-3

Interior & Cover Illustrations: Evgenia Barsheva

Book & Cover Design: Lazuli Literary Group

LAZULI LITERARY GROUP
home of *Otherworld Realism.*

otherworld realism
[**uh***th* -er-**wurld**] [**ree**-*uh*-liz-*uh* m]

noun

1. a style of literature devoted to intellectual and imaginative pursuits that point towards a potential, evolved reality.
2. a genre that represents the known, often mundane world in an elevated or defamiliarising way through the skillful use of linguistic craft, innovative language, or experimental structure; contrast with **magical realism**, which integrates choice plot elements into a conventionally accepted reality.
3. art and literature that evoke the space before clarity in which one must navigate the logic of intuition and instinct, alongside the duplicity of fact.
4. an approach illuminating a psychic space of process; a space of ambiguity, silence, and internal struggle.
5. the pre-dawn.

Word Origin
2017; coined by Lazuli Literary Group; first appeared in *AZURE: A Journal of Literary Thought, Volume One.*

TABLE OF CONTENTS

BISMILLAH
(from "Three Disintegrated Sonnets for Abbas Husain, MD")
by Abby Minor

Bright light, persimmons wrapped in paper, vent-
ilator, scrubs: *To say the time of death,*
to say this person's name out loud, to toss
a shaky knife at the moon. *It became*
a very silent practice, spinning out the spark
of smile in someone else's eyes…

                                    Abbas,
I'd like to write full sentences for you,
to place the taste of water—common, strange,
unburnt, unmasked (the after-mask)—but bright
the history of medicine, and bright
your children's names, and bright the crayfish you
caught as a kid. I heard you say *fever*
cough, short of breath; fever, cough, short of breath
and thought of persimmons that ripen, coaxed:

little orbs, little flames: and names,
(I will not let you go) and names.

IF YOU WERE ALL WATER (AND YOU MOSTLY ARE)
by M. Ann Reed

If you were all water (and you mostly are) Alpine pure, gentle as dandelion seeds, strong as hummingbird inspections, their beaks pointing at your third eye, mistaking for a moment your face for a sunflower, you would remember as well as any elephant every electromagnetic spectrum communication you've ever overheard. You would remember what a deep freeze you made of Walden Pond during Underground Railroad winter days, your depth of ice thoroughly measured by Thoreau, and you would remember those light waves of joy from liberated feet crossing over you spreading their exhilarating breaths of bliss. And if you were one of the liberated, you would know—oh, Honey, you would know—it was your time to bloom! You would feel the surging life force unfurl your never-before goldenly proportioned spiral of Amaryllis petals, the truth of the one and only you born to spread diversity, creating real unity spoken by your petals in their various dark velvet appearances similar to, yet not the same as, others wearing night's equity into day. And that yellow spark of light in your eyes, scattering seeds, planting trees, reorganizing cells until the shining pours out of your skin—that yellow spark of light would be pollen radiating the dust of your new star—

THE LOOKING GLASS OF ARTHUR GORDON PYM

by Frank Meola

New-York, August 1838

It is with some reluctance but compelling need that I set pen to paper once again on the subject of my recent voyage into the southern Pacific Ocean and the narrative relation of it first published in the *Southern Literary Messenger* under the name of Edgar Allan Poe. Mr. Poe, editor of that publication, learned of my adventures and encouraged me to set them down, trusting that my awkwardness of style would testify to the veracity of my account. But I was hesitant. I did not believe I could write from memory a description that would convince the reader. Poe therefore suggested he himself write the narrative, or a part thereof, and publish it in the magazine as fiction. This ruse would demonstrate that the story's facts would be believed by the public even though presented to them as fiction! And indeed this is what occurred. The narrative was taken by many as truth. Consequently, I decided to write my own description of the entire adventure AS FACT, there being evidently no danger of the public not believing it was all true.

And so *The Narrative of Arthur Gordon Pym of Nantucket* was published as a book, edited to the point of extensive re-writing by Mr. Poe, who nonetheless took great pains to assert the authenticity of my story, allowing me, for instance, to write a preface explaining the genesis of the work. We had discussed it over whiskey in a series of dingy taverns in Richmond, Virginia; afterward we would make our slow way down the narrow streets in a sort of alcoholic haze of delight and terror. The details of my horrific ordeal had all come back to me in waves, and Poe obviously re-imagined them, vividly, almost as if he'd lived them himself. For the results of our shared intoxication—liquor and fantasy mingling—was a tale full of exaggeration, even though I recalled hewing close to the facts, perhaps somewhat colored by my state of mind.

Furthermore, over the next several weeks the book began to sell (modestly) and was received by reviewers and public alike as entirely the work of Edgar Allan Poe, based on the factual account related to him by me—that is, by Arthur Pym. My dismay at this turn of events, my feelings of betrayal and usurpation, were nothing compared to a far more powerful feeling: that of obliteration. This was my text, this text was my life, and now it was another man's text and life—no, worse, I was now the invention of this other person. I was, in effect, dead. One could say murdered. For I discovered (too late, not having read the final proofs or the finished book with all its emendations) that Poe had added a long note after the narrative's last page, the page on which I describe the "shrouded human figure," enormous and white, that rose up before us as our boat plunged into what seemed to be a giant cataract. The note began thus: "The circumstances connected with the late sudden and distressing death of Mr. Pym was already well known to the public through the medium of the daily press."

Sudden death! Well known! Imagine my horror at reading these fraudulent words. What could have been Poe's motive in writing them? I was (I am) quite alive and well, despite the nervous condition brought on by my terrible ordeals. I immediately sought out Poe and found him in another dreary, dank pub, inebriated but entirely capable of reasoned discourse. He explained—as we shared a drink—that this postscript was another ruse: my putative death would serve to reinforce the truth of my existence. His slight Southern inflections lent an ironic melancholy to his words as he regarded me closely with that intense, haunted yet mischievous gaze. I stared back, suddenly dizzy from the combination of drink and bizarre paradox. I found myself drawn into those bleary-sharp eyes, almost as if I were falling, body and mind, into their depths.

Perhaps noting my distress, Poe reached over and touched my arm, as if to reassure me that I was as solidly real as he. His face relaxed—as much as it ever relaxed—into a sardonic smile.

"My dear Pym," he said. "This need not pain you so much. I have told your story. Everyone believes it is true."

"But, sir, it is true!"

"Of course, of course. But the public wants a fable, they crave the fantastic. At the same time they want to believe it's all fact. They want reality as a story."

"Yes," I said. "I can see that. Yet when I read it, it feels like a dream of my experience rather than a memory."

"I am not sure they differ. Dreams like memory have imposed, often fanciful meaning. People crave meaning. We all want to see the symbolic significance of things. To read the hieroglyphic, as it were. Just as you did in those island caves in your story."

"In my reality," I replied. "And I could *not* read them." (He was referring to the caves on that island where we encountered the natives near the narrative's end.)

"In your reality, no. That is my point. I have attempted to provide those things people want but do not find in the quotidian."

His words were persuasive, like the rhetoric of a performer or a confidence man. I had begun to assent again—no doubt partly an effect of the liquor.

"Beyond all that, there is benefit to both of us. More in fact to you than to me."

"How is that?"

He leaned back, gave a terse, almost harsh laugh.

"I am gaining some renown. I hope to reach a larger public and thereby improve my precarious circumstances. Relieve my debt."

"And I?"

"Well, you too will earn some money. But you will also gain a second life."

I stared. He seemed, for a moment, crazed.

"A second life," I repeated.

"Yes. Your life is now my book. Our book. But you are the person living in it, the voice of its apparent reality. I am merely its author."

I found myself nodding in agreement, at first timidly, then eagerly. I realized it was exactly what I had wanted when I entrusted my story to Poe. I had come so close to death repeatedly. I felt a strange desire to be alive in a different way. A less vulnerable way.

"But there is a certain price for this," Poe continued.

"A price?"

"Yes. You see, in order to exist thoroughly and permanently in our book, you should disappear."

I pointed out that I did disappear at the end of the story. The narrator, that is.

"No, I mean *you* should disappear."

My enthusiasm drained away, replaced by a dread that seemed to rush up from a fathomless pit. I could not speak.

Poe continued: he was aware of my utterly solitary life, my nearly total anonymity. It would be a simple matter for me to go on being, as it were, dead. I could retire somewhere, there were so many secret places in this vast country into which a person could vanish, metamorphose from one life into another, become a different person. With a different name.

"But my name is Arthur Gordon Pym."

Again Poe laughed. I had of course spoken the first line of my Narrative (Poe's line).

"Yes, yes, certainly," he said. "But that name must now become a fiction, as it were. You can invent another."

I felt as if the shabby floor had opened up and I was falling. Steadying myself, swallowing another whiskey, I forcefully objected to Poe's suggestion, which sounded like a command, as though he was in control of my actions—indeed, at this point, of my existence.

There was little mirth in Poe's laughter nor in his sad eyes. He repeated that he was offering me immortality, that my formless real-life adventures required his shaping mind, his powers of reverie and ratiocination, to become the kind of fantastic (yet true) tale that might work its way into the nation's mind like some collective dream. There it might remain for generations, with my otherwise quite humble name attached to it.

"And of course your own name," I said.

"Of course." This time his laugh withered into a near sigh, as if the thought of this renown, this nominal continuance through time, potentially into some far unknown future, pained him as much as pleased him.

The deflation of Poe's spirits oddly calmed me, and I once again began to reflect on my good fortune at having survived, at being alive at all. Surely that was the important thing: I was robust flesh and blood, far more so than this shriveled, sad author sitting across from me. Yet I had no prospects. I had in fact inherited a goodly sum from my father, thanks to his wise investments in Edgarton New Bank stocks, but because of my prolonged nervous condition upon returning from the South Seas, it had been necessary for me to support myself entirely with those funds. They were dissipating quickly, given the comforts I indulged in as a means of calming my stormy mind. Indeed, part of my motivation in (reluctantly) attempting to write down my adventures was financial.

And I had always desired to distinguish myself, to demonstrate to my skeptical father that I was capable of great things. Alas, I was a failure in all respects save in the circumstances of my life at sea. In the recounting of those circumstances I might be a hero. Of course, my father was dead and so in a sense would I now be.

I assented to Poe's proposal; we shook hands. His, like mine, were trembling. He suggested an attorney in New-York who might effect a name change and handle Poe's periodic payments to me. It would be a good place to be anonymous, New-York, Poe wittily suggested. No need for obscure places. Hide in plain sight. Be a man of the crowd. I concurred.

I actually grew to enjoy my living nonexistence. Contrary to my (Poe's) statements in the first chapter of my Narrative, I have no close family and very few friends. None, sad to say, so much as noticed my disappearance or, if any did, they preferred not to take the trouble to inquire or report about it. I moved my few clothes and possessions to a small but comfortable room in the City Hotel near the southern tip of Manhattan. I passed most days walking the streets, filled with a vibrant mixture of humanity. I relished the notion that I was a sort of ghost among them, observing them, known to no one. Fully there yet invisible—one among the democratic crowd, as Poe had suggested.

At night, however, lying in my unfamiliar hotel bed, my brain teemed with phantoms, horrifying and outlandish images—some of them vivid memories of my arduous voyages, others weird and fantastic distortions of those memories (as in my Narrative). On waking, it became difficult to tell them apart. What had actually occurred? Poe had spoken truth: like dreams themselves, our memories are reconstructions, retrospective approximations. We make meaning of our dreams when awake, and we do the same with our memories of reality.

Yet there must be a distinction.

And so I want to revisit key episodes in my adventures, as I think they happened, not as Poe recounts them. I will try to focus on actual occurrences, things observed directly through my senses, not augmented by dream or imagination. I feel that these re-creations, these notes on what Poe wrote, would be closer to the truth, coming directly from my memory. In this way I hope to calm my feverish mind and so achieve more restful sleep, even if no one else reads these pages.

I want to rectify, for example, the false impression that my friend Augustus had smuggled me aboard the whaling ship *Grampus*, and that I had hidden myself below decks during the entire course of the bloody mutiny, of which I was completely unaware until Augustus informed me of it. This is preposterous, because in fact NO SUCH PERSON REALLY EXISTED. It was one of Poe's more audacious inventions. If the reader consults Chapter Two of my (that is Poe's) Narrative, the following passage can be found at the end of the first paragraph: "Augustus thoroughly entered into my state of mind. It is probable, indeed, that our intimate communion had resulted in a partial interchange of character." Oh, the ingenious Poe! How he thus both disguises and reveals his true intentions, his attempt to appropriate my identity and distort (while enhancing) my story. Note what he says several sentences earlier: "My conversations with Augustus grew daily more frequent and more intensely full of interest. He had a manner of relating his stories of the ocean (more than half of which I now suspect to have been sheer fabrications) well adapted to have weight with one of my enthusiastic temperament, and somewhat gloomy, although glowing imagination." There are several implications. First, that Poe and I are in some sense doubles, that in telling my story he has imbibed my character and I his, a phenomenon he expresses through the invented person Augustus. The second, more disturbing, suggestion is that I faked large portions of my narrative, that I am a fraud, even though it is not a narrative in any fictional sense; it is my actual life, albeit in the words of Edgar Allan Poe.

Here is the truth: I myself set forth on the *Grampus*, and I myself was a victim of the horrendous mutiny, held prisoner in the fetid bowels of the ship, without food and with minimal water, for several days until, through my own efforts, I escaped. I then formed a connection with one of the mutineers, a line-manager named Dirk Peters, and gradually we devised a plan to re-take the ship from the more radical rebels, who wanted to abort the voyage entirely and return home.

Who is this character of Augustus then?

I have found an answer in the narrative itself, odd as it was to be searching an account of my own life for clues to the true nature of the people and events in it (my life, I mean). You will perhaps recall the incident not long after I befriended Dirk Peters when we decided to terrorize the other faction of mutineers through my disguising myself as a shipmate who had recently died, most likely poisoned by another crew member. I dressed myself up as the dead man, painting my face to resemble that of a corpse. The scene in which I observe myself in the mirror is only slightly exaggerated; I do recall distinctly the delicious sensation with which I beheld my dead face or, rather, experienced myself as another, dead. Looking at me, a reflected disguise. It was this dizzying confusion of self that seized me, producing not only fear (as Poe asserts) but a sort of delight. And then the trick itself—the thrill of anonymous power, as though I were supernatural, combined with a magician's bliss at creating awe and wonder and fear through illusion. Falseness taken as fact.

I perceive a direct link between this scene and the later death of my "friend" Augustus, in Chapter Thirteen. Since Poe persuaded me to declare in my preface that I took over the narrative, I at first believed that he alludes there to his own "disappearance" from the story. But I re-read the latter parts of the work and was reminded of how fantastic and bizarre the story becomes, with its gargantuan polar bears, seas white as milk, murderous dark-skinned natives of fanciful islands, and near-starvation leading to atrocity. I daresay all this clearly flowed from the feverish pen of Mr. Poe, infusing my New England story with Southern grotesque and, surely, a Southern dread of Negro insurrection. Obviously I had little to do with these lurid descriptions.

Again, here is the truth: we did experience horrendous thirst and hunger, and we did encounter exotic, combative islanders in the southern Pacific. But there were no massacres and, emphatically, WE DID NOT RESORT TO CANNIBALISM. I would certainly have died rather than participate in the repulsive ritual described (thankfully in a brief and vague manner) by Poe in Chapter Twelve. Our shipmate Parker died of fever, induced by famine, and we gave him a proper burial at sea, with Christian prayer, quite the opposite of the heathen horror described by Mr. Poe.

All of which leads me to the conclusion that the character of Augustus is based not on Poe but on myself, and that it evinces Poe's desire to kill me (as it were) and take over my story. Which he did, voraciously. Indeed, the story as it unfolds beyond the death of Augustus follows only the outlines of my actual adventures; this is a voyage not only into the Pacific but—more forcefully—into the imagination and vision of Poe. Into some transformed world. I cannot have actually journeyed there and experienced those outlandish things. Which is to say that the character of Arthur Gordon Pym must actually be Edgar Allan Poe.

But who then am I?

I can only be the *real* Pym. The one who actually survived. And who has now died and has been living on in different forms, anonymously in the New-York streets and with a new name in this room I now inhabit while my former name attains a kind of immortality in that book by Poe.

But of course I died before. Because, you see, the ending—which puzzles so many—is the one aspect of the second half of the story (after Augustus' death) that is substantially true. We did sail through strangely opaque water, although it wasn't milky or warm as in Poe's description, and we did continue on south, through more and

or night, there arose that vast white curtain as I (Pym, Poe) depict it in the Narrative's last pages, that cascade of whiteness like a glacier dissolving and plummeting in crystal fragments. And, yes, we did plunge directly into that cascade. It is the last thing I remember of that journey.

What actually happened? We were rescued, saved, by a British ship. Implausible, I know, but true. At least true according to others. I awakened—after intermittent episodes of semi-consciousness on what was clearly a boat—in a Lon-

more mysterious and wondrous regions as we approached the Antarctic. But I fell ill during that last part of the voyage; an odd sort of lethargy came over me as we drifted toward an eerie horizon of pale daytime sky, nights brilliant with stars and flashing many-colored light, all the while surrounded by the icy sea. And suddenly, one day

don hospital. I was told that I had seemingly died and had been perilously close to following poor Parker into burial at sea before suddenly displaying evidence of life.

I would go further. I believe that I actually died, briefly, and that the white cascade was the boundary of life, death's portal, through which

I passed, only to return, filled with awe and terror. And a deep sense of the sublime. Since then, I have felt daily, in some recess of my mind, a strong desire to cross that boundary again.

Here the ms. of Mr. Arthur Gordon Pym breaks off. Evidently Pym never wrote the full revision of his (Poe's) narrative he had planned but left only these few pages sketching his intentions. My name is Dirk Peters, and I am the custodian of this remarkable letter to posterity. As the letter reveals, I too survived that all-but-incredible voyage. For a long time after our return to America from England, I had no contact with Pym. Perhaps neither of us wanted to be reminded of our dreadful if marvelous experience by being in one another's company. Also, I was living in Illinois and Pym (I believed) in Richmond, Virginia, so our paths did not cross. However, I recently received a note from him, asking that I visit him in New-York, where he was now residing. There was something very important he wanted to give to me. He also informed me that he had been living under a different name; his odd explanation for this was a desire for fame through his book without the burdens of fame in life. I was reluctant at first to see him again, but curiosity and a fellow-feeling born of extraordinary shared adventures at last compelled me to make the long trip.

Imagine my shock at finding out that the New-York address Pym had given me was that of the Bloomingdale Lunatic Asylum, in the wild northern reaches of Manhattan Island. Upon inquiring at that grim establishment, I was told that Pym (who was calling himself William Wilson) lived among the milder cases, in a private room on the third floor. His physician (a gaunt, pale man who seemed to blend with his white smock) was at first reluctant to discuss my friend's condition, but I convinced him that Pym (that is Wilson) had no close family or friends, and that he had expressly requested to see me. The doctor explained that Pym suffered from a neurasthenia perhaps induced by some horrendous ordeal, manifesting itself as inertia with episodes of delusion. He sometimes, for instance, believed he was dead, only masquerading—so to speak—as

a living man. He was otherwise quite lucid, however, and no danger to himself or to others. He'd been ejected from the City Hotel when he took to sitting out on the sidewalk, staring blankly and referring loudly to the hotel as "a charnel house." A kindly woman from the hotel had brought him, passive and unresisting, to the asylum.

The doctor's explanation overcame my initial alarm and I followed him to Pym's small room, where Pym and I were permitted to speak in private.

He sat at a desk, looking out a window toward the Hudson River a few streets west. He turned and greeted me, using my Christian name. I had expected an enervated, wasted figure regarding me with crazed eyes but Pym was quite the opposite. He stood and walked serenely toward me, hand extended, and we shook.

"I am happy you came," he said.

"How could I not?"

He asked me to sit in a chair next to the desk and resumed his own seat. We exchanged some inquiries about one another's health and lives but did not delve into shared memories. After awhile, Pym became silent and turned to his desk. He took up a handwritten document and offered it to me, explaining that it was a copy of a vitally important response he had written to his own narrative as written by Edgar Poe. He wanted me to keep the copy in the event that the original was damaged or lost. As the only other person with a major role in the events described, I should be the one to be the document's guardian.

I asked if I should read it. Of course, he replied, but he preferred that I wait until I returned home.

He smiled slightly. "I too will be returning home soon," he said. "Though I don't quite know where that is yet."

There was something mysterious and vaguely frightening about this statement; he seemed both eager and resigned at the thought of that "home."

I left him still sitting at his desk, once again gazing at the river, that majestic estuary of the bay and sea.

I read the document upon my return to Illinois. And I quickly understood that Pym was indeed delusional or perhaps some combination of delusional and deceptive: he had re-imagined some of the most horrific events of our journey (accurately rendered by Mr. Poe), ennobling and taming them and making himself their hero. At the same time, he had endorsed some of Poe's wilder exaggerations, notably the shrouded human figure appearing at the end of the narrative. This re-telling of occurrences indeed revealed a mind that could not cope with reality. I can certainly understand why Pym might not want to face the extremities to which we were forced, especially the eating of human flesh. But we did in fact engage in that dark ceremony of survival, and Pym's denial of this fact created in me a sense of solitary guilt and savagery, a feeling that I was not human. Or that Pym was attempting to exclude from the human those baser impulses Christian civilization (as we call it) would prefer not to acknowledge. That I am what Poe terms a "hybrid" man made these feelings all the stronger. My Indian blood and my participation in mutiny put me on the "savage" side of those questionable distinctions Poe insists upon toward the narrative's end. Poe misrepresents the violence as entirely perpetrated by the South Seas natives, while Pym turns away from the violence altogether.

Here are the facts (I am a simple man, not given to deceptions): Pym was trapped in the ship's hold throughout the mutiny, and he continued to conceal himself there, aided by his good friend Augustus. The assertion that Augustus was invented by Poe, a fictional element in the narrative, is utterly absurd and further evidence of Pym's current state—a sort of delirium, a moving in and out of fantasy. (Rather like that state he—that is Poe—describes in Chapter One, wherein Augustus is utterly intoxicated yet appears lucid and rational.) Both Augustus and Pym helped carry out the plan to take the ship back from the renegade faction of mutineers. Pym indeed disguised himself as a corpse or ghost to terrify that faction, a deception in which he took a strange sort of enjoyment.

Our journey to the remote southern islands and our adventures there among the native population occurred in a manner much closer to Poe's version (of Pym's account) than to Pym's re-writing of it (which would seem to indicate that Pym related the events to Poe in that original form). There were skirmishes, there was bloodshed; we had come into those islands as frightening pale invaders with mysterious weapons. As for the cryptic chasm writing, none of us ever deciphered it. Poe's attempt exactly to reproduce that writing on the pages of the book is surely a playful fraud.

And the curtain of white at the narrative's end, well, I did not see it as Pym describes it: for me it was a wall of ice or an effect of southern light or some other quite natural phenomenon. The sea did appear oddly colorless, but not milky white (or warm) as in Poe's description. Of course, Poe seems obsessed by whiteness.

But enough explanation. I am amending this note to the document Pym gave me, and I shall place both in a secure location in this home on the prairie, far from the sea, where I hope to live a long life amid family and friends—putting my wonderful, terrible adventures in the past. I will not spin those adventures into stories; I am no literary tale-teller.

To the readers of the *New York Tribune*, August 1900:

I found the above accounts in the Illinois home of Mr. Dirk Peters while doing research for my novel *A Strange Discovery*, about Peters' life after the events so powerfully described in Poe's *Narrative of Arthur Gordon Pym of Nantucket*. My name is Charles Romyn Dake, and my novel, recently published, is in fact a somewhat fanciful relation of my search for Dirk Peters as well as a truer account of his further adventures with Pym. Since the truth of my entire book has been challenged, I feel the need to explain. In reality, I did not find Peters myself; early in my investigation I learned that he had recently died. But the family living in his former home (not his own family) kindly allowed me to follow an intuition and search the home's musty cellar. There, in a long-neglected corner, sat a box labeled "Grampus"—the sort of box that would have been stored in that ship's hold, where Pym lay for so long in hiding. Inside were three documents: the two above (Pym's letter and Peters' note) and another, much longer manuscript by Peters—an account of his and Pym's later journey to an island near the South Pole called "Hili-li." On this latter narrative—too lengthy to be reproduced here but in my safekeeping—I based my fiction. I am aware that Peters makes no mention in his note to any further adventures (nor does Pym), but Peters' manuscript is presented as a true account and I have no reason to doubt it.

I know that questions will be raised about the authenticity of all these documents. I will likely be accused of fabricating them in order to defend my work and increase public attention to it. Naturally I considered the possibility that these were inauthentic, perhaps someone's playful attempt at making fictional characters appear to have been real persons. I even entertained the notion that Mr. Poe (known for his literary joking) had composed them—and presumably hid them in a basement in Illinois! But these possibilities seem absurd. It is true that I did not meet Peters in the flesh, but I assure you there is ample evidence of his existence. Augustus Barnard and Arthur Pym are harder to trace. The former name appears in records and in many New England memories, although there is no certainty that this is the Augustus in question. Pym, however, seems to have been erased or to have erased himself from the world. Not even the Bloomingdale Asylum has a record of him—neither as Pym nor, oddly, under his assumed name. I obviously believe he—and Peters and Barnard—actually lived among us, even if I have no definitive proof.

My work, like Poe's, is a true account of actual events, in fictional form. I offer these documents as evidence of my veracity. Believe them or not. They are genuine. The men who wrote them are as real—were as alive—as I am myself.

(END)

CONTRA FORMALISME

by Leland Seese

---

shaggy raggy rudeboy hip hop feministic slam
starchy Formaliste is up in arms

Formaliste insist on platted streets & tuckin shirt & tuckin sheets
but heat's too heat for shirt & sheet a'tall

Formaliste knock wrong way talk wrong color
lovers with wrong other   Formaliste give mouth-closed
kiss-o, *mwah!*

Formaliste too tight to be cool head

Truth — sez Formaliste police — perpetual pentameter
never swivel rhythm equatorial & never poor no queer no brown-o

                never from the rez

Formaliste must nullify free verse-o soon as
it come strummin outta angel-headed hipster angel head

knock 'em out & 'speare 'em   manacle   exclude
deter   then *civilize*

by step on everybody else's neck

RODION RASKOLNIKOV ON HOW TO SURVIVE A PANDEMIC

by Leland Seese

after *Crime and Punishment*
by Фёдор Михайлович Достоевский

I have a hatchet.

A hatchet can be used

to split

wood and populations

infinitives and skulls and ideas.

Some of us deserve to live

through this pandemic.

But what's the sin

in excising from among us,

say, old lady pawnbrokers?

Or, just old ladies? Or

just the elderly and feeble?

Maybe I should peddle this

in Texas. Or maybe I should

lay my axe aside

and kiss the earth in penitence.

OPIATE CONVALESCENCE

by Leland Seese

———————

Morning fadey, filly, fally, folds of black and gray.
Scattered papers must be stamped for passage. Flaccid hands
are dampened chamois ribbons in a car wash, slap, slap,
slap at documents.

Awake, he finds he's in the time-zone of his birth.
Fog-soft morning weighted underneath a quilt
of culpability.

Getting home a desperate press, slog through slough
and muck and milfoil, eyes fixed
on the light, a shifting pinprick, tiny star,
wander, waver, weave in distant galaxy.

Ignorant of energy expended until the journey's past.
Waking ready for familiar. Finding
there's no going back.

He sees a bridge remembered from the inbound trip.
Rumors it was ruined in the interstice.
But there it is, his heart a sunrise, bright eyes,
thrown down unexpected gullies.

Hopeward, then, to brim to find the bridge has vanished.
Scabrous plain all accusation. Fingers flutter
as the agent coughs derision at his heritage.

Painfully-raised head from stony pillow
as if Jacob, out of joint forever, remade as disabled.
Longing longingly, long
journey home.

FOSTER PARENT HAIKU

by Leland Seese

This poem cut short.
A call from CPS. Please
take this child tonight

BLUES ON RED

by Elie Doubleday

Inspired by Marilyn Chin's "Blues on Yellow"

Robin breast crest plumage pledge worn on my sleeve
Robin breast crest plumage pledge worn on my sleeve
Robin breast crest heart pledged sleeve for thieves

Red picked raw, pocked peeled fingers burnt with worry
Red picked raw, pocked peeled fingers burnt with worry
Red and raw, rocked and reeled, my fists that burn with fury

Rose petal skin, highways on arms raised raw and aching
Rose petal skin, highways on arms raised raw and aching
Petal soft skin raised raw blemished but fading

Pink lady picked down from the apple tree, red peels off to white
Pink lady picked down from the apple tree, red peels off to white
Pink lady picked fresh from the apple tree, pale flesh revealed and light

Blood runs red in blemished veins; fingers remember to write
Blood runs red in blemished veins; fingers remember to write
Blues run red, life punches ahead and bruised I remember to fight

INTIMATE THINGS
by Laylage Courie

CHARACTERS

HELOISE
ABELARD
SWELL HENRY, a man played by a woman.

PLACE

ACT I: *The Dialogues of Heloise & Abelard*
at the Paraclete
An imaginary lecture/demonstration.

ACT II: *Sic et Non*
A lecture with interruptions.

ACT III: *Indeed words were few*
A lonely man at a bar.

TIME

The suspended present.

SYNOPSIS

What does life look like once passion is past? Swell Henry descends from his 21st century mountain height—the top of the Empire State Building—to tell his troubles to an empty bar.

NOTE: Text printed in all caps is excerpted from Betty Radice's translation of The Letters of Abelard & Heloise *(Penguin Classic Edition, 2004; revised by Michael Clanchy). Abelard's parables (*) are extracted from his treatise* Sic et Non *as translated on the public domain bibliofile site.*

ACT I

The Dialogues of Heloise & Abelard at the Paraclete

(SWELL HENRY appears to be the Director of this play who for budgetary reasons is also the stagehand.)

(The stage makes some small pretense of being an austere rhetorical school/convent in 12th century France. It is possibly set only with chairs and microphones, in the form of a panel discussion, along with, as example, a garland of fake roses, a small gothic arch resting on a table-top, a color print-out of a religious stained glass window on a folding easel or... etc. ABELARD might enter, ask SWELL HENRY for water. SWELL HENRY might bring two plastic cups on a lunch tray, along with a cheap wine bottle wrapped like a basket. He imagines the bottle is a rustic earthenware jug. It is the best he can do.)

(Etcetera.)

(ACT I's context might not be understood until ACT II, if then. Not knowing exactly what is going on should be enjoyable for all.)

(The titles of the scenes are important and should be part of the production.)

Scene One
HE PLAYS THE LION IN HIS HOUSE

(ABELARD is alone. HELOISE enters.)

ABELARD

Let us sit facing the sun. I like the sun in my eyes. With the sun in my eyes, the present, now, becomes golden. Like a memory. The sun will not always fall so fully on our faces: forehead, cheeks, collar bones, or, permit me to observe, décolletage. What fine wrists. I like. The way the sun suggests. I sprawl. With indifferent languor. Like a beast.

(HELOISE sits.)

(End of Scene.)

Scene Two
SHE CANNOT BE EQUALLY WITH MEN AND GOD

(HELOISE speaks to ABELARD without looking at him.)

HELOISE

He says: "A part of you is always alone." Isolated, immune, removed, distant, alienated, separate, detached. Faraway. Solitary. Cut-off. Deserted, desolate, remote, estranged, at-odds, divided. Uninvolved. Indifferent. Impassive. Shut-down...

18

ABELARD

Maybe...

(HELOISE looks at ABELARD.)

HELOISE

I'm not alone.
I'm just not with him.
I'm with someone else.
Inside.

(ABELARD nods.)

(End of Scene.)

Scene Three
SHE HAS SLIPPED OFF HER DRESS

(HELOISE speaks to herself. ABELARD is not listening.)

HELOISE

This is where the story begins. Here. In this room. Finding the dust and lost change beneath the mattress, behind the bed. I won't toss what I find. I will spit on it, murmur a few magic words, and shape it into a beast. A beast with the power of a lion and the grace. Of a winged horse. I will tend her. Lovingly.

(End of Scene.)

Scene Four
NIGHT AFTER NIGHT ON HER NARROW BED SHE SEEKS TRUE LOVE

(HELOISE and ABELARD speak to each other.)

HELOISE

I feel like a girl who has come to tell her father some thing. The thing is precious to her but as she begins to speak it, she feels ashamed.

ABELARD

Because it is wrong?

HELOISE

Too precious to speak?

(Pause.)

ABELARD

May I ask if you experience problems of a sexual nature?

HELOISE

Yes. Oh yes. But. Not really.

(Pause.)

ABELARD

Would you say you feel incomplete or unfulfilled? Needy or insistent? Empty? Or unsatisfied?

HELOISE

I would say I feel hungry. With a hunger no man has the imagination to fill.

(End of Scene.)

Scene Five

THE HEAVENLY BRIDEGROOM TORMENTS HER WITH TRIBULATIONS

(HELOISE speaks to SWELL HENRY.)

HELOISE

We don't discuss it. No. It is simply chained to our legs like a feral dog.

(End of Scene.)

Scene Six

THE IMPORTANCE OF THE PROBLEM IS MATCHED
BY THE SUBTLETY OF HIS SOLUTION

(ABELARD speaks to the audience. HELOISE listens.)

ABELARD

I want to talk about "imagination." I want to talk about what I imagine at night. I imagine trees. Very old trees. Common trees. Oak trees poplar trees sycamore. I imagine a tree's life in reverse. I imagine: twigs shriveling into branches into trunk. Filament roots sucked back into the tap. Solar flares, dirt, rain hurl as a century old tree is compressed into a sapling, a sapling standing like an adolescent, arms lifted towards heaven at the still hole in the center of a hurricane—before it is sucked back into the earth.

The winds settles around upheaved ground. Where a seed nestles. A seed nestles in the earth.

Explosive.

(End of Scene.)

Scene Seven
FROM THE ENDS OF THE EARTH HE CALLS WHEN HIS HEART IS IN ANGUISH

(HELOISE speaks to ABELARD.)

HELOISE
Do you dream about the wind? Do you dream that the wind tears through your hair? Lifts your arms and parts your legs? The wind smears your face against your skull. You look like a satyr with your face smeared against your skull. You are lifted. On your back. The stars whirl nearer, nearer and you laugh. You double over, laughing. Doubled-over, you are too heavy and you fall. You smash against the ground. Then something else. I can't remember. A departure. A going forth into darkness. Along a path so smooth I think it must be paved with water.

(End of Scene.)

Scene Eight
THE MORE HE POSSESSES THAT WHICH CAN BE LOST
THE GREATER THE FEAR WHICH TORMENTS HIM

(ABELARD speaks to the audience. HELOISE listens.)

ABELARD
I used to dream of water. Flood. The walls of the oratory rising like cliffs around a lake where the pews are drowned. Fish leaped before the altar of the fisher of men. Drowned birds dredge the alcoves, butting against mold-blackened saints. Boatmen engage in for-profit ferrying up and down the aisles. Rats scramble, snouts poked above the flood. Paddling rats. You don't think that's funny? Rats scurrying in water against a torrential flood? The faithful clambering up the bas-relief? Dangling from arches like clusters of grapes? Garlanding the pointed windows like a profane host? I'll admit I hesitated to love anyone. Whenever love rose in my body, yes, like a flood, I remembered that everyone—especially the everyone that I loved—would die. Love. How do people bear it? Forget "betrayal." Forget "separation." Even "the Best Scenario:" a "long-and-happy-life." Ends tragically.

It was hard, knowing that, to embrace rapture with all-welcoming arms.

(End of Scene.)

Scene Nine
THE TONGUE IS A SMALL MEMBER OF THE BODY
BUT HOW VAST A FOREST IT CAN SET ALIGHT

ABELARD

Tell me about him.

HELOISE

About sleeping with him? I liked it.

ABELARD

Trying to sleep with him?

HELOISE

Yes. I'd like that, too. Yes.

ABELARD

Because it would take a long time.

HELOISE

I'd like his hands on me. Their furiousness. Their increasing furiousness. Their desperation.

ABELARD

What does it feel like.

HELOISE

Stillness in the center of a hurricane.

ABELARD

No it doesn't.

HELOISE

Yes it does.

ABELARD

A dry wind through blanched grasses.

HELOISE

(Pause.) The rustling wind across open fields.

ABELARD

Like that. Exactly.

(End of Scene.)

Scene Ten
HE LOOKS ON WINE WHEN IT GLOWS AND SPARKLES IN THE CUP

(HELOISE smokes.)

HELOISE

Would you like one?

ABELARD

I like that your lips don't leave stains on the cigarette tip.

HELOISE

I don't rouge my lips.

ABELARD

Yes. That's why there are no stains.

HELOISE

Why don't you just say "I like that you don't rouge your lips"?

ABELARD

Because I wouldn't mind if you did rouge them. I like that when the cigarette comes out of your mouth, it is unsoiled. Moistened. But white.

(End of Scene.)

Scene Eleven
SHE DISDAINS TO RISE FROM THE BED OF HER CONTEMPLATION

(HELOISE speaks out while ABELARD listens.)

HELOISE

Shall I tell you of my only love? Who interrupts my dreams? He interrupts he is gold and husked. I peel the husk. He feels good in my hands. Sun-warmed. Thick. Silked and sticky. Kernels pop between my teeth before he plow tills the field, its ridge in the furrow grind of some god beneath the belly from the slashed stalk splitting its sheathe. I am unsheathed for dawn scattering its kernels of gold from the sky into the bed into the womb.

ABELARD

That bloody animal.

HELOISE

Yes.

(End of Scene.)

Scene Twelve
HE GATHERS EACH BLOSSOM AS IT COMES TO MIND
AND CREATES A SINGLE BUNCH

(ABELARD speaks to the audience. HELOISE is not listening.)

ABELARD

This is where the story begins. Scraping fluff and coinage from my pockets, shaping them with spit and a few magic words into an animal. A magical beast. "This is my life," I say. The virility of a satyr. The fierceness of a bull. The wise inconstancy of a centaur. Ah Bacchanal! This is the story I tell. This is the myth I make.

(End of Scene.)

Scene Thirteen
WHOEVER SITS IN SOLITUDE
SHALL HAVE ONLY THE HEART TO FIGHT AGAINST

(HELOISE and ABELARD look out.)

HELOISE

Are you unsatisfied? Discontent? Saddened? Lost on the tumultuous winds? Are you equipped for the journey? Are you without compass? Have you lost your sense of direction? Sex? Life?

ABELARD

At night. Before the sun is set. Twilight.

HELOISE

As the sun is setting.

ABELARD

I wander. Windows illuminated before curtains are drawn. I see the colors of walls. The decoration of rooms. I've never once seen two people kissing. Twilight, as the sun sets, don't you want to sit close with someone dear in your arms? As the day, the whole day, departs? And kiss them? Kiss them as the last glances of light are thrown off interior mirrors like the reflection of passing birds?

HELOISE

You walk the streets.

ABELARD

At night. Curtains drawn. On the streets. I look at the trees. Two hundred years old. Lining the streets. Their girth. The wondrous complexity of their branching. I run my hands along their trunks.

HELOISE

I saw two people kissing. They looked at each other with heavy eyes. His hand was inside her blouse. I could see the cotton crease and stretch and rise.

Her legs parted as if she had forgotten them. Her eyes were as heavy as water. I saw a girl once. She stood before her uncle. She looked at him, then at her knees.
He sat at his desk with his back to her.

ABELARD

Did she want to tell him something?

HELOISE

Was that the day she found blood on her thighs? There are several reasons for that, aren't there? Some of them a girl wouldn't tell her father about, would she? What would he think of her?

ABELARD

He would feel sad for her. He would feel sad because he would feel the pain of the whole world rushing towards her like thousands of sharp knives.

(End of Scene.)

Scene Fourteen

ALTHOUGH HER BODY IS CLOISTERED HER MIND STILL LOVES
THINGS OUTSIDE AND PURSUES THEM

(HELOISE speaks to the audience. ABELARD is not listening.)

HELOISE

What do I like?

A resonant voice. Sounding like the drum of hands on hollowed wood.

Strong hands. The hands that could hollow a boat or a drum out of wood. Hands that can do delicate work with simple tools.

The look on a man's face when he's doing delicate work. When he's concentrating.

I like a man who is sure in the water. I like to see arms, chest, breaking the surface of the water. The line of the water at his hip, at his thighs. His body, surfacing. The light breaks off his body. He shakes his head. Glass is thrown. I weep. Oh penetrating beauty. How can I ever hold you? I will never hold you. I weep for such temporaries. Glass in my skin. In my eyes.

What do I like?

A man who can stand at a threshold. Step over that threshold without hesitation. As necessary. As it became inevitable. Not without sorrow. With dignity. I like the man who, when he hovers at a threshold, looks back, for only the fraction needed to sign, beyond all words: Good bye. Fare well.

My only love.

(HELOISE looks at ABELARD.)

(End of Scene.)

Scene Fifteen
ALWAYS THEY SEEK THE FORBIDDEN AND DESIRE WHAT IS DENIED

ABELARD

Tell me about your friend.

HELOISE

The nun and the philosopher obscure themselves in robes of night.

ABELARD

(Furious.) This is where the story begins. Where we take the fluff, lint, coinage of our days and make of them some kind of myth.

(End of Scene.)

Scene Sixteen
SHE WOULD RATHER BE EXPERIENCED IN BED THAN SEEN AT TABLE

(HELOISE and ABELARD face off.)

ABELARD

Ravish me.

HELOISE

A fantasy.

ABELARD

If you will.

HELOISE

A man in a garden. I can tell a lot about a man from his manner in a garden. Does he stroll purposefully, or meander? When a flower is fragrant, in what way do his hands lift a bud to his mouth? The way he asks if I'd like to sit. Does he lead me, or merely offer? Is he assured? Does he try to please? His command of the situation.

ABELARD

Shall I tell you what I am like?

HELOISE

What you yourself are like?

ABELARD

Of course. The woman with me. This makes a difference. Imagine, for instance, it is you. It is late afternoon. Autumn. The light is gold at the edges of your hair. It is warm and you wear clothes like that.
That fall open. I am aware of the bare skin beneath your throat. Perhaps I do not notice the roses. Their
fragrance. I am a man of intention. I watch you. You cross your arms. You smile, generously. Such a
generous smile. I say "Will you sit on this bench for a moment, where the last light falls?" You answer…
what do you answer?

HELOISE

Yes.

ABELARD

And you sit, right in the middle of the bench, and I do not know where I should sit. So I sit in front of
you, positioned to look out, into the cool, gold light, and also at you, surreptitiously. I speak concisely but
my attention, really, remains on you. The distance between us. It is not so large because I am tall when I
sit. If you will but stay, leaned forward, with your elbows on your knees, I think I would like to touch two
fingers to your chin, lean in, and kiss you. I intend it gently but, alas, I kiss you and. My body. Suspends.
It is as if a stone hits the pool of my body, here, at my solar plexus, and from that here I ripple out.
Suspense. Suspend. Exquisitely. I kiss you. Your ankles uncross and my knee slips between yours. Such
languor in your body. Your body falling open. Softening. The languor of breezes in meadows. A woman
being kissed. You. Kissed.

HELOISE

Your eyes. Gold-edged in the light.

ABELARD

Your skin, beneath the lines of your clothes, cream.

HELOISE

Stay with me. Stay.

(End of Scene.)

Scene Seventeen

ALL MIRACLES ARE PERFORMED EITHER IN LONELY OR IN HIDDEN PLACES

HELOISE

If only.
Your mouth…

ABELARD

Shhhh.

HELOISE

...here.

ABELARD

It is time to go.

(End of Scene.)

Scene Eighteen
AN EMBRACE IN THE ARMS OF FAITH
FOR HE WHO ACTS DIVINELY IN THE GLORIOUS FLESH OF A VIRGIN
WHICH HE ASSUMED FROM THE PARACLETE

(Silence.)

(The distance between HELOISE and ABELARD and.)

(The space between their bodies.)

(The shape of the space between their bodies.)

(More present than they are.)

(HELOISE exits.)

(End of Scene.)

Scene Nineteen
DO YOU NOT KNOW THAT YOUR BODY IS A SHRINE
OF THE IN-DWELLING HOLY SPIRIT?

(ABELARD, in HELOISE's absence, speaks to the audience.)

ABELARD

Love without language. I will tell you about her body. I will tell you about her body as I lay her on the bed. Softly. As if she were a girl. I lowered her to the bed. The sheets were gold. Her body was white. The color of milk. Her hair. All over her body. Dark. The white rocks of the river dark with algae. No. Love without language. The long shapes of her legs. As they opened. Opening. Parting. I parted them.

28

My hands gentle at her knees, along the inside of her thighs. Yes. Love without language. I will tell you about her body. I will tell you how her hips lifted, her back arched. I will tell you about her breasts pushing upwards as her head fell back. I will tell you about her hair between my fingers on my tongue in my mouth. I will tell you about her eyes when she was lost. How deep. The depth of her eyes as her mind died and she was only aware of her body. The depth of her eyes, dark, bottomless, instinctual. Let no man go there. Let no man. But we plunge in. We cannot help ourselves. We plunge inside. And I held her to me. I pulled her close into my chest. These are the mysteries. These are the mysteries. Love without language. I will tell you. I will tell you about the dark places. The dark places when the soul inhabits the body. The deep places, then, in our eyes. When her eyes close, she sleeps. What is it dies? Endlessly? Endless? What is it? Inside?

(End of Scene.)

Scene Twenty
THIS IS NOT OFFERING A KISS BUT PROFFERING A CUP

(ABELARD re-lights HELOISE's cigarette from before.)

(Smokes.)

(Stubs out.)

(Exits.)

(Ash in a dish on an empty stage.)

(From which smoke rises.)

(For a long time.)

(End of Scene.)

END OF ACT I

ACT II

Sic Et Non

(SWELL HENRY lectures. ABELARD listens. HELOISE is not present.)

(SWELL HENRY displays supporting exhibits on a screen. The exhibits will become less and less relevant. The Empire State Building should eventually appear. See Act III.)

SWELL HENRY

Abelard and Heloise lived in Medieval France. He was the greatest logician/philosopher of the 12th century. She was renowned in her own time for her knowledge and understanding of classical literature. Abelard seduced Heloise when hired by her Uncle as her tutor. When she became pregnant, he secretly married her and stashed her in a convent, where they continued to have passionate rendez-vous. When Heloise's Uncle discovered he had been deceived by the formerly celibate scholar in his own house, he hired henchmen to castrate Abelard in his sleep. There ended Eros between Heloise & Abelard. He became a monk, she, a nun. Their letters begin some ten years later, after Abelard spent a brief time serving as the Father Confessor to Heloise and her nuns at the Paraclete—the school he founded and later gave to Heloise for her convent. The letters begin with a letter from Heloise to Abelard full of longing, anger, and betrayal. She claims Abelard had not spoken personally to her the entire time they co-habited at the Paraclete.

ABELARD

In love you will float. In a small boat. Over unfathomable depths. A lake silver brimmed to the horizon. But allow. Allow yourself to rise. From the lake's surface. Its shore will become apparent. Its silvery surface will grow smaller and smaller, until it is resolved into a coin. Engraved with a boat. In which two people are vaguely supposed. To sit.

SWELL HENRY

In love you will float. In a small boat. Over unfathomable depths. A lake silver brimmed to the horizon. But allow. Allow yourself to rise. From the lake's surface. Its shore will become apparent. Its silvery surface will grow smaller and smaller, until it is resolved into a coin. Engraved with a boat. In which two people are vaguely supposed. To sit.

ABELARD

I WOULD WRITE MORE THINGS TO YOU BUT A FEW WORDS INSTRUCT A WISE MAN. INTENTION IS ALL AND INTENTION IS LACKING. INDIFFERENTER (INDIFFERENTLY) SCIBILITAS (KNOWABILITY). SIC ET NON. WHAT MORE?

LOGIC HAS MADE ME HATED BY THE WORLD. THE STORM MAY RAGE BUT I AM UNSHAKEN THOUGH THE WINDS MAY BLOW THEY LEAVE ME UNMOVED; FOR THE ROCK OF MY FOUNDATION STANDS FIRM.

SWELL HENRY

The coin can be treasured, pocketed, stolen, lost, or spent. It is evident that love must be drowned in or resolved with this perspective. It is impossible to float tranquilly upon it for long.

Afterwards, what? Dive back into the deception with someone new? What "real thing" remains once passion has died, the lake is demoted to coin? In his letters to Heloise, Abelard says "God". I can't blame Heloise for her frustration with him. It is possible she had seen Abelard only once after her Uncle's henchmen castrated him in his sleep. When he signed her into a convent. Imagine that: Heloise, the abbess and a sister or two, meet Abelard in a small receiving chamber. Abelard is in a state of shock. Heloise represents his humiliation and shame. She is "she-who-I-can-no-longer-fuck." He thinks, at this time, that a eunuch befouls the eyes of God. His humiliation and self-disgust must be extreme. Any glance between Heloise & Abelard is as intense and as forsaken as the glance between Orpheus and Eurydice. As I imagine it, Heloise is both Orpheus & Eurydice, Abelard the mirror in which she glances at herself. The act of being seen by her beloved as no-longer-beloved is violent for her. It is the moment that her life is severed, her passion dismembered. Abelard's dismemberment preexists his meeting Heloise. The loss of Heloise is merely a symptom of the violence. His inner turmoil obliterates any other emotion. He is not really in the moment, the last moment, with her. He cannot be. He is in shock. She sees, through him, herself drawn into the underworld. Heloise, looking back at her beloved who no longer sees her as beloved, sees herself, sinking from the earth through soil into the land of shades. She takes her vows. Before him, because he did not trust her to go through with it.

The knife's cut, for Heloise, is not clean. Passion was full in her mouth. Pried her jaw open and snatched it away. Unlike Abelard, she is hungry.

When Abelard replies to Heloise's first letter to address her "old perpetual complaint against God concerning the manner of our entry into religious life" he uses erotic metaphors to describe the nobility of her cloistered life. Heloise's lover is no longer Abelard, it is the Lord. How blessed is she! A chunk of Letter 5 analyzes a Canticle about a European King's Ethiopian wife. Her black skin looks less lovely, but is soft, subtle, and loveliest to experience in bed. The Ethiopian bride—Heloise's soul cloaked in the outwardly unattractive life of a nun—is the superior consort, most pleasing in the bed of the Lord. Heloise has entered a sacred chamber where she is sublimely embraced by the Lord. Abelard humbly addresses his Lord's bride. The eunuch serves his master's queen.

I laugh when I read Heloise's response. She nobly agrees to restrain herself from continuing complaint. She instead humbly petitions Abelard for advice on convent "Rules": what clothing and underwear should sisters wear suitable to their fragile bodies and menstrual cycle? Should sisters offer Christian hospitality to men and eat at table with them or is that inviting temptation? She asks, too, if sisters should drink wine given it "encourages sensuality". Yes, I project my preferred subtext: I don't want Heloise & Abelard to slip too easily into cloister banter. He responds to her plea for personal discourse with lofty sexual metaphors about "knowing" God? She asks him to consider what she wears under her habit, her volatile libido. Knowing, as we do from his letter, what his "uncontrollable desire did" with her in the "corner of the refectory" dedicated to the "the most holy virgin" while Heloise was disguised as a nun, ("I, repeat, you know how shamelessly we behaved on that occasion in so hallowed a place," writes Abelard), her questions are sharp.

Nevertheless, it isn't titillation I look for in the *Letters of Abelard & Heloise*. I read to know what they meant each to the other when passion was lost to them. Abelard addresses Heloise as his "beloved", "once dearest to me in the world, now dearest to me in Christ." Is this deep-seated feeling or proper style? Letters of the period (according to the introduction) were always written in a grandiose, literary style. What do his addresses signify? I am alarmed by what reads as estrangement. What comfort does Abelard draw knowing Heloise prays for him as he endures heresy charges, book-burnings, and assassination attempts? "I can find nowhere to rest or even to live; a fugitive and wanderer I carry everywhere the curse of Cain, forever tormented..." he writes. When accusations against him peak, when "logic" makes him "hated by the world," he writes a confession of faith to her. It feels urgent, almost personal. Abelard trades erotic Heloise for Heloise-the-sacred-bride. He expects her to intercede on his behalf on judgment day. "A man's wrongdoing will be wiped out by the entreaties of his wife."

Heloise? Did Abelard's presence always dwell quietly beneath or above or within her practical and scholarly work? Did her love diminish in intensity? I imagine that it did, that time brought perspective. The lake, if not a coin, became a pond that her life flowed into, then out of, on its way to the sea. Perhaps she found quietude after his death, when news of him, words from him, or even his arrival were no longer possible. Her heart, full of longing towards nothing of this earth, slowly emptied itself of worldly passion.

It is desirable to imagine that for both Heloise and Abelard, a meta-reality co-existed with the trials and details of their daily lives, and that each could retreat to it. This meta-reality undoubtedly contained a presence they called God, but it also contained an image of the other as soul's mate traveling parallel towards a single vanishing point, a familiar to be finally met in the here-beyond. It is tempting, necessary, to imagine this.

I read Heloise and Abelard to learn how the soul loves beyond Eros. My edition notes that both were familiar with Cicero's De Amicitia, a treatise which founded an ideal relationship of "disinterested love". Both Heloise & Abelard believed in an ideal love of devotion, "disinterestedness" that transcended marriage and eroticism. Reading that, I am irritated. When the erotic element is lost, their relationship drastically changes! I want these great lovers to instruct, not on how the ideal is lived abstractly across time and space sublimated in the fantastical bliss of eternal union, but humanly, viscerally, embedded in the everyday real. I wish Heloise & Abelard had lived more intimately or written more often. I am disappointed that they do not teach me how the soul's love, after passion, dwells humbly, deeply, and contentedly, in our common world. They do not tell me that love of the soul dwells humbly, contentedly, in our world.

ABELARD*

I will open my mouth in parables.

It is a noteworthy quality to love the truth in the words, not the words themselves. For what use is a golden key if it cannot unlock what we desire? And what is wrong with a wooden key, if it can unlock what we desire, when we wish nothing but to open what is closed?

Although there is no place in the entire universe that is entirely empty and not filled either with air or some other body, still we say that a box in which we perceive nothing by sight is empty.

If there be anything left, you shall burn it with fire.

A sentence is true if things stand in the way it says, and things make sentences true or false in virtue of the way they are, and nothing further is required.

(SWELL HENRY turns off his projector. While he puts on his coat, these words appear on the exhibit screen. They are cast by a projector held by HELOISE, standing in the audience. SWELL HENRY does not see HELOISE or the words.)

(Projected words, one line at a time:)

A TRICKLING FONT.

BASIN SMOOTH AND UNADORNED.

HELOISE (GARDEN) SPLASHED UPON.

WHOLE, GLISTENING, SPLASHED UPON.

HER CALF, CROOKED OVER RIM, SWINGS.

LIKE A CENSER.

ATTAR OF ROSE. WORMWOOD.

LISTEN AGAIN PLEASE: THE TRICKLING FONT.

STUTTERING SPILLAGE AS

SHE EMERGES.

HELOISE.

HEAD BOWED.

SHE EMERGES (BASIN)

HANDS CLUTCH RIM
BACK ARCH REVEALS

WINGS
(HERS)

FEATHERED WITH STONES.

TREMORING. MONSTROUS AND IDLE.

ABELARD
(Calm.)
Hand towards hat plumed with swords. Draw. Advancing.

HELOISE'S SONG
(Singing:)
Nominatissima,
choose shoes soled thin as eyelids
I implore you to the chapel at dawn.
Then will bed reveal what my heart now hides.
Let the sweet fountain of yourself bubble forward
Who can deny you are buried in me?

(SWELL HENRY exits in his coat.)

(ABELARD, on stage, looks out at HELOISE, in the audience, holding a projector of light.)

ABELARD
LO I ESCAPED FAR AWAY AND FOUND A REFUGE IN THE WILDERNESS. I TOOK MY-
SELF OFF TO A LONELY SPOT I HAD KNOWN BEFORE. A tree pierced the sky like a ragged
thorn. Memory is the most treacherous tempter, reverie mangling austere practice. Purity is allotted only
to our bones.

ABELARD	HELOISE
(Calm:) MY LOVE, WHICH BROUGHT US BOTH TO SIN, SHOULD BE CALLED LUST, NOT LOVE. I TOOK MY FILL OF MY WRETCHED PLEASURES IN YOU, AND THIS WAS THE SUM TOTAL OF MY LOVE. MOURN FOR YOUR SAVIOR AND REDEEMER, NOT FOR YOUR CORRUPTER AND FORNICATOR. IT WAS HE WHO TRULY LOVED YOU, NOT I. FAREWELL IN CHRIST IN CHRIST FARE WELL AND LIVE IN CHRIST.	*(Blank shouting:)* MY LOVE, WHICH BROUGHT US BOTH TO SIN, SHOULD BE CALLED LUST, NOT LOVE? I TOOK MY FILL OF MY WRETCHED PLEASURES IN YOU, AND THIS WAS THE SUM TOTAL OF MY LOVE? MOURN FOR YOUR SAVIOR AND REDEEMER, NOT FOR YOUR CORRUPTER AND FORNICATOR? IT WAS HE WHO TRULY LOVED YOU, NOT I? FAREWELL IN CHRIST IN CHRIST FARE WELL AND LIVE IN CHRIST?

HELOISE

Love is a black river that runs towards death. The waters are cold and dark. Only a beast could cross such a river. We are not delicate, strong enough. The water is too cold. Too swift.

END OF ACT II

ACT III

Indeed Words Were Few

(SWELL HENRY enters a bar near the Empire State Building.)

(SWELL HENRY removes his coat.)

(He selects a bottle and a glass from the bar, then sits.)

SWELL HENRY

(A toast:)

Oh my radiant sunrise oh my radiant sun. She has four thorns. Four thorns radial from the wheel of her mind. They crown her like rays emanating from a Madonna. She is not a Madonna. The thorns are her own. Her hair as red as blood. From the four thorns? No. She has placed the thorns carefully. She does not bleed. Her smile is sad but her eyes are as calm as oceans.

(A toast:)

Oceans.

(Soliloquy:)

I hear the wind. Not swiftly. Not in gusts. Continuously. It does not let up. The wind tosses tin airplanes and boats. It tosses bits of paper and sea froth. It crosses vast distances. I hear it because I am born-in-air. I am born-in-air and I hear the wind blowing, not just around this building, through these streets, but high in the stratosphere. Because I am born-in-air, my heart is an aircraft with a small, straight beacon light, navigating up there. In the winds. I am that insignificant. That insignificant and that free. Tied to nothing. Tossed in turbulence. Blown through sky. What a joyous thing is man! Buckled in his little tin can, tossed in the unnavigable, indifferent wind. On his way. Somewhere.

Of course the tin can has wings. That's why one can laugh, one can go-with-the-flow, so to speak, having wings.

Tonight I'm a real cloud stopper. Did I say that? Did I say cloud? Crowd? Crowd pleaser. I'm a real pleaser of crowds. Here's the bottle. And the glass. And the bar.
Have you noticed that no one's tending the bar?

(Calling out:)

There is no one tending the bar!

(To Audience:)

If you come up here I am not going to make your drink.

No. I do not golish plasses or drix minks.

(To self:)

Did I say that?

(To Audience:)

I do not do those things, I'm saying. I sit here. At the bar. With a whole bottle to myself. So I don't really need a bartender. I'm a pleaser of clouds. A real cloud pleaser. Clouds cross vast distances, oceans, on the great winds, to hover over me. The winds. Hear them?

(Pause to listen.)

They are very high. You can hear them particularly at the top of a tall building. The Empire State Building, for example, which, I believe, is still standing. Right over there. Is it still standing? Yes. I believe it is. It is standing. And—as I was saying—if YOU stand at the top of it and if it is not too crowded and if you aren't too tired or. If you are. Very, very tired. You can stand very still on the top of it and feel it moving, every so slightly. Swaying like a woman imagining a dance from a long, long time ago.

No. That's not how it sways. It is not introverted, it does not sway inside itself. It sways against an outside force. Yes. The Empire State Building sways—as I was saying—against the wind. You can hear the wind there, if you are still and tired or not very tired and there are no clouds. I mean crowds. You can feel the subterranean hydraulic shifts balancing one thousand four hundred and fifty-four feet of steel, glass, duct work, office furniture, plumbing and wire, against the force of air. You can feel the shifting under your feet. You can see the view—the pan-o-rama, so to speak, move. An engineering feat. Vertiginous. And—as I was saying—you can hear the force it adjusts to. You can hear the wind. Constant. A wordless breath. Not menacing. Just indifferent. Just terribly terribly forceful and indifferent. You hear it and you are apt to feel, surely, that you have miss-stepped. That you have tread on inhuman, therefore sacred, ground. You were not meant to stand here. To be this high. You are a mere man, meant to stand, awestruck, beneath the altar of the cathedral, looking up in wonder at its nether reaches. Only great men—Master Builders, Michelangelo—are meant to stand at the tops of cathedrals. Because God—or whatever—is supposed to dwell Up There. But here you are, higher than any cathedral, with a touch of vertigo, watching.

The clouds swiftly pass.

The sun, that ancient clock, arc.

The city sprawl over three states.

The Atlantic crash over the horizon.

And you don't hear God. No. You hear the wind. Do you hear it?

(Pause for listening.)

You know what's worst? No one's painted the ceiling for you. When you stand at the top of the Empire State Building and look up, the beauty of the archangels does not take your breath away. No. Your breath is punched out of your gut. If you fall to your knees it is out of sheer dizziness, not awe. Survival instinct yanks your gaze out of the wild blue yonder before you are lost. Forever.

Did I say that? I can't believe I said that. It is a phrase, a phrase out of Gone with the Wind. Or something. It is a ridiculous, melodramatic phrase. Can you be lost, forever? Wouldn't you eventually stumble upon some place you'd been before? Or your soul. Your spirit. Can it be lost forever? No. I do not think so. If it lasts forever. If that, then it will find its home there. It will find its home somewhere in forever. Or it will be where it is and not want to be anywhere else and so it won't be lost anymore because it won't want to go anywhere. Or.

(SWELL HENRY looks up, falters, and falls to his knees.)

Ver-ti-gi-nous.

(He clambers back up.)

And now, ladies and gentleman, a real cloud stopper: The Staircase Genius. Who has a pair of dice. He is flanked to left and right by winged, radiant Madonnas offering safety nets like chalices to the sky. Beneath him there is ocean, and above him, the sun circles and falls, agelessly. Above him, high, high above him, the sound of the wind.
The sound of the wind not speaking, not calling to him.
No. The wind:
>born out of pressure and solar flares
>pulled pole to pole, magnetic north to south
>cooled over fissured ice fields
>run rampant over the unhindered plains
>pushing eastward across great lakes, mountain ranges
>to the eastern seaboard
>the wind, I say, whipping towards the Atlantic

snags its hem on the nails of New York where loose threads of it gust through the street corridors. This is where the Staircase Genius begins his climb. The Staircase Genius staggers back. But he is not discouraged. Yes.
No. The silliness. Wind. Cloth. Let the wind be as it is. Irreducible. Unrestricted by metaphor, cathedrals, skyscrapers. Hear it.

(Pause for listening. SWELL HENRY regroups.)

The Staircase Genius hears the wind. Bracing himself, he casts two dice on the stair. The number: three. He leaps three sheets to the Three steps into the wind. He picks up the dice. He casts them. His life is a baffling dream.
The stairs go up up up insurmountably. The sky is radiant and then it is dark, in quick succession. Sometimes he is blinded, and sometimes, in darkness, he is blind.

The genius of the Staircase Genius is that he does not despair, he does not fret, as he climbs this kind of stair. The Staircase Genius looks up up up straight into the sky and when he does so he does not fall to his knees and he does not suffer from vertigo. He sees the sun, crossing. He notes its position. His eyes blink with the modesty of straightforward calculation. He looks at the stair immediately before him and casts his dice. With the efficacy of an engineer. He leaps forward.

(Fierce, to self:)
But I, I am born-in-air. I cast my dice against the wind and leap after them. Perhaps I will fall to the ocean. Perhaps, I will ascend, toes pointed like a saint's, face radiant like an idiot's, into the yild blue wonder.

Did I say that?

(Cold resolve:)

Then what will now happen is: the liquid I have drunk from this glass will, as I tilt my head back to drink… flow, in slow motion, from my mouth back into the glass. When I lower the glass to the table (as if lifting it in reverse) I will already be holding the bottle directly over the glass. The liquid will waft, like a genii, up from the glass into the bottle. When I set the bottle down, it will be full. A miracle. The evening will go backwards. Oh my radiant sunrise oh my radiant sun she has four thorns four thorns radial from the wheel of her mind…and so forth, in reverse. Everything. Backwards. Backwards. Until…

Until?

Were I saint this bottle will be full. Were I idiot it will full, though you might only see the fool, dribbling spit down his chin. But in truth? Though born-in-air, if I leap after the dice, the wind will blot me against the sun like an apparition for an instant only. Then, I will fall, a clot of earth, out of the sky. The bottle will be empty.

(Toasts:)

She has four thorns four thorns radial from the wheel of her mind. They crown her like rays emanating from a Madonna. She is not a Madonna. The thorns are her own. Her hair as red as blood. She has placed the thorns carefully. She does not bleed. She does not bleed. Her smile is sad but her eyes are as calm as oceans.

(A toast:)

WHATEVER A LOVER GIVES TO A LOVER, WHAT MORE?

(A toast:)

INDEED, WORDS WERE FEW.

(To self:)

BUT I MADE THEM MANY BY RE-READING THEM.

(He is going to toast again, but the bottle is empty.)

(He considers the bottle.)

(He tries it…going backwards: he lifts the empty glass to his mouth. He lowers the glass to the table, lifting the bottle back over it—the gesture of drinking/pouring in absolute reverse. When the bottle is again poised over the glass he stares intently at the space between them with excruciating hopefulness: for a moment he believes liquid will rise back into the bottle.)

(Speaking the following is arduous at first, but builds in speed and eloquence, making some kind of sense:)

SWELL HENRY

By many them made I but few were words indeed.
More what lover a to gives lover a whatever.

Oceans as calm as are eyes her but sad is smile her bleed not does she bleed not does she.
Carefully.
Thorns the placed has she blood as red as hair
her own her are thorns the Madonna a not is she
Madonna a from emanating rays like her crown
Mind her
Wheel radial thorns four thorns four has she
sun radiant my
oh rise sun radiant my
oh

(Stillness.)

Love is a black river that runs towards death, that black tree charring the sky as if lightning slashed out of the earth. Purity is allotted only to our bones.

END

LOVE LETTER TO LANGUAGE: AN ABECEDARIAN

by Saramanda Swigart

Agate autumn evening in bed, inside me verbs unfurl, fernlike fractals
Becoming new branches, leaf-words strewn or gathered, brindle, a typesetter's
Case overturned, lead letters littering the ground to collect, coalesce into rich-man
Dreams, sumptuous as cinnamon, textured as dimpled damask, soft-rumbling as an
Engine; English lets me step into her like a bath, a new skin, my mama's voice
Forming the florid hazel forest of Yeats' Aengus, who pursues inspiration, a
Girl with apple-blossom hair, chased through lands dappled, golden, hilly,
Hollow, but he never has her, the pursuit itself a heady headlong hagiography.
I love my language as a lover loves, how it—sultry, soft, delicious, dazzling,
Jocund, joyous, morose, milky, bursting with birdsong, moist in the mouth—
Kabooms and careens and moans and murmurs and morphs to fit any mood
Languorous at times—at times bombastic, a marching band—or bare as bread
Metastasizing on the muscle of its own inner intricate yeasts, massing up into the
Numinous night air, a nacreous cloud cover above the city that hums with the
Opals and pearls that are (now) verses falling into a lover's ear, the delicate Byzantine
Pulchritude of her shell-like organ, word-potpourri behind a gauzy curtain, how
Quixotic that I yearn to—not hear exactly—but *feel* those words enter her, those
Rotund letters, Bs like breasts, like all a woman's protuberances, patter of Ps up the
Spine, sensuous, sibilant, a snake charmer's syllables, drawn up to the mouth by the
Trembling, reedy plaint of speech; in another home, words a trap of tar, a child's terror,
Uncanny dreams hanging upside down in his curtains, flap and fluster over his
Voice, small in the bed, praying, surrounded by plush, insufficient protection, night a
Watershed from which he will never return the same; for peer into any body,
X-ray for taxonomy of bone—tibia, tarsal, fibula, phalanges, cranium, carpals, ischium;
You see they are made of words, erected into forms, then feelings, then figments, the eternal,
Zealous reshaping of chaos into patterns that we lose control of the moment they are born.

DRUNKEN MAN ON A BICYCLE

by D. S. Butterworth

1.

A drunken man on a bicycle tumbles over streets
like a crumpled paper in the wind of history—
behold the miracle of flying trash, animal
shapes rich and strange: top hat horse head,
dinner jacket monkey, ferret and weasel
dealing five-card stud at the conference table—
marvel at the polished sheen of this inscrutable
now. Step right up: watch the raveling
of the feral woman, witness the juggling hands!
For we have decreed sacred this manner of inebriation,
this monkey riding the back of a dog, godlike,
our adorations gathering as insect clouds
over the muddy waters of our borders, malarial,
heretical. Hush for the conjuring spell, marvelous
prestidigitation! For we have canonized this chaos
of handlebars, this zigzag careening through
the morning commute, this hit and run of spectators
frozen in testimony, infectious—maybe you, maybe me,
as the turning of the bicycle weaves
and veers to eat the world up.

2.

Look: the mind's windy places, secret
and wandering, fill with antic shadow,
with flotsam from underworlds of blood
and hunger, as a sham fury seizes synapse
and cell, contorts the private spaces
into marketplaces, into dread and trivial theater
drawn with chartered streets where once sang
lullabies of winter and moon, now doodled
apocalypses with clown horns and shoes.
We watch the shadows prance across a screen
and marvel as a gun becomes a magpie,
death a mouse in motley, the machine of state
a bicycle, Lord Chaos, a drunken man shape-
shifting as the wind of the mind drifts and palls.
Step right up, Ladies and Gentlemen, one and all!
We are the sad and rapturous Americans,
gunpowder connoisseurs, rubes and dupes, suckers

and sages, traitors and patriots, the enamored crowd,
brutal and incredulous, furious and mad—

3.

He rides the wind from his own mouth
as it fills invisible sails
of rumor and conspiracy,
fictive worlds blooming in his wake,
fleurs du mal, algae eating up the oxygen
in the self-same pond that is his mind—
O Kingly brain—creating one ocean
of self, receptor agonists and neurotoxins
alike declaiming verses in prophecy,
silken parachutes
of circus tents
to bless elephants and giraffes,
dressing the chimpanzees in ballroom
guise, colonizing our cerebellums,
whip, cane, scourge, and flage,
(Poor Tom's a-cold)
with cartoons of dung and arsenic.

4.

The theater loves its monkey: electric
child, darting over the skull's furniture
climbing the starlit dome, tiny proscenium,
on rumor of storm and war from the far pavilions.
Our vervet nervously picks the teeth of a baboon,
smoothes the strings of the puppet with affection.
And suddenly a new birth—Imperial Decree—
eats up our thoughts, affections, dreams, the day's
little plans and comforts, swallowed in the shadow
of billowing tent as the monkey whimpers for
the pony-riding dog, for giraffes straining
their alien faces against the radiation from facsimiles
of bellowing clowns, the famed performers, purveyors,
sleights of hand. The theater loves its monkey,
the dimensions of its secret rooms,
the music of everyday, voices from the garden,
applause for the clever quip, the committee table
triumph, the saucepan victory. But read in the eyes
the fixed attention, imagining the rousted salute,
the cartoon report drawn in blood, artillery echoing
through the hills of the approaching weather.

November is the cruelest month: Run Monkey, Hide!
The lever you pressed for candy now delivers shock,
but you keep pressing to burn, to weep and burn and mock.

5.

The man on the bicycle believes he is America.
He rides the cities and plains, intoxicated.
Maybe like me, maybe like you,
he climbs the ladder of weeks, a clown
on a wind-up scooter with a wheel that limps.
He imagines he is hauling bones of enemies,
but they are the ribs and femurs of a king in a sack,
but they are heavy and wheeze as he rides,
but the sack is his body and the bones are his own,
but he steers toward a shiny bauble at the curb,
a silver rattle he can shake to remind
himself that he is king and scepter of the world.

6.

A tide of faces rises on his screen, a field
in spring after rains, before drought. The child
he carries inside climbs his ribs astonished
that so many have traveled to Earth from
whatever stars to peer out of these hollow
eyes of oxidized bronze. Bells ring down
the beginnings and the endings as time
rages above the faces in tongues of flame.
He surveys tombs of men who ruled and died,
of women who ruled and died, and painters
who rendered the gestures and motions as women
and men: naked or nun, impresario or clown.
Maybe he's them, maybe he's us. Maybe this
is metaphysical theater he mistakes for simple
circus, Punch and Judy, the awkward puppets
splayed beneath loosened strings, where
he points to the fire-eater, the contortionist,
illusionist and knife-thrower—and we ask, Daddy
what are those men doing behind that curtain?
He says: don't you want to see the naked lady too?

7.

The child inside him squeezes the man's heart
in his hands to drain the darkness. *Where greatness?*
he asks and scans TV Guide. Now the child covers
the bicyclist's eyes from behind and the whole
balancing act teeters, a stone street trapeze,
Tiresias's eyes blinded by a naked Venus of himself,
as if careening through this flood of faces he might
extinguish the image. But no, pyrotechnics flare,
the child's hands a miracle of loaves and fishes
scattering across mall and piazza, the crowd's accordion
dilations like birds flocking in wind over the river
to avoid the magic bicycle as it casts spells
and curses, a hanged man rattling in the spokes.
The drunkard rolls beyond control through
an old banker's heart, through pockets of merchants,
ledger books of bloodwork paid in gold and silver.
He fishtails through sodden plaster, through crowds
of pilgrims along the muddy river and over
the stones that are the body of civilization as it sleeps.
He wobbles like an Etruscan, almost driving
into their same dark soil with their words and gods
a cumulous contrail behind his metal horse.
Besotted with his sole self image naked and devouring,
his great star rises and sets beyond wisps of hair-like cloud.

8.

The drunk on the bicycle is America and its king,
is the crowd and ghost of crowd, he is the sleeping
part of the mind, the ranges where geometrical
shapes of urge and fallacy swim in amniotic darkness,
Babylons of desire, Jerusalems of memory,
the lace and stone corners where birds and apes
have gone haywire in imagination's mausoleum.
The bicycle steers its own course through a hall
of mirrors where etched script traces stories
of the plagues—here a map scorned face and tribe,
there stands a man in tin where the blood and flesh
wrung out long ago, here demons wore a path
over mountains, there demons mowed the villages,
as if to say these are the yourselves you used
to be, you walk the streets to dream and sing
in the emptiness: *me my little self am this I*
an animal singing in the new world's reliquary.
The bicycle weaves through a Gettysburg

of becoming and dreams itself as the only tin, the only
aluminum facsimile of candleflame in the damp cellar
of dark-swallowing light reborn as acetylene torch.

9.

A clown on a bike! We laugh, we cringe, we cry,
what can go wrong, we wonder, moments before we die.
His elliptical motions a delirium, his huffing
breath spawn of words as cartoon monsters,
squadrons of machines, bristling with missiles,
famine and war bursting like thought bubbles
from the burlesque of a body as it weaves. We thrill
at the force of the man as a bicycle morphs
into tank and turret—but is it in a dream he flicks
battalions from his shoulder with a sneeze? We
only see the syphilitic jester, the chimpanzee
bullying his way to the front of the line with daddy's
swag, for the imponderables of the child
in the control room configuring himself as a man
who scratches an itch at his back with whole economies,
sneering at entire cities as if they were mosquitoes,
knocking over forests like Alamos in a game of skittles,
for the horror drowns into a whimper. The bicycle
of the imagination steers like a fish in air,
unstable, insecure, a wavering gaze,
a stumbling clutch of smoke, inebriate, debauched,
surfing on the contempt pumping through his own heart
so full of gasoline it blinds him to the pure sway
of stasis, to the still point he might find and hold,
and delivers him into the inertia of asteroids in orbit.
Maybe you laugh, maybe you cry, maybe you sleep
and dream: no body forgets how to ride a bike,
the taste of candy, the thrill of circus tents billowing
in the wind of childhood—Mommy, why is the Ringmaster
grabbing the trapeze lady, why is he falling down?

10.

And now all the mad people are speaking into their hands:
Behold the colored whirligigs above the Congress,
the painted horses galloping in a ring!—here
a Bush stepped on a stone, there a Kennedy
combed her hair, look at the way that façade shapes
the sky, how the dome becomes massive against
the storm of change. Now the crowd raise their hands

to prove they were here before the world was free,
and now they turn their hands to carving
a nation into sunlit chiffons, now they wrestle demons
into the earth, death by drowning, death by arrow,
death by sword, death by edict, death by directive,
death by mercury and arsenic, death by demon air—
beautiful death by ink sluiced off newspapers
into tinctures of anger and confusion, death to all
but the immaculate self, tax-less and finally free—
what a show. The biggest crowd ever.
Voices rise to hail the invention of a new
mathematics, new words blare like bassoons
and charters and decrees to spin it all up
in a giant cocoon so they can give birth
to freedom as dark matter, ink the intoxicant
free from words, free from meaning, free
from anarchist's slogans, free like machines
with wings, like monkeys with leathern wings
chattering across a cobalt sky. The drunken man
on the bicycle follows his wheels where they
lay tracks of a new language weaving through mud,
a new tongue twisted into dark screens
as a Babel of people speak into their palms
where ghosts have gathered according to the spell:
O let us drink the moon and light our way
with candles and follow a trail of wax
as the wheeled contraption cranks
the drunken man home—all ye all ye home come free.

11.

A Napoleon in motley, a Medici in rags,
a Machiavelli of the people. His wheel razes
crooked roadwork stones—let us number them
so we can re-assemble the puzzle the way some
Khrushchev or Goebbels, some Stalin or Mao
will recognize as history's inevitability. Let us dream
some deep chemical architecture of a new nation
to fresco over the ashes of memory. Pace the towers
of the Khan, O Senator, prowl the towers of the inebriate
King, O Congressman, pace the broken crenellations
and scout for rumor from seas, pace the battlements
beyond the rising rivers, beyond waters pressing the wall,
cheer the siege with saltless foes, grind the enemy's
palaces to dust, destroy the narcotic televisions,
burn the veils of silk, strafe the caravans and turn the sand
to glass. Read the flight of crow, the fire's ash, augury

of tea leaves in the cup, prophesize gold in futures
of arsenic and polonium.   Trade alphabets like pilgrims,
cast the Phoenicians and Greeks into a copper pit,
bargain for astrolabes to navigate the bays, climb
the profit sheets on a ladder of ribs cured
from the carcasses of your slaves, piss on the agonies
of the old wars the piss of vodka and gasoline,
hammer failed hope into a facsimile of a horse
in tin and ship it to an antique market, stamp a dull dollar,
florin, or ruble and awaken the muddy river of your America.
Rise again like matin bells flaring over the rooftops and sing
our past to parchment, powder the eggshells, spit on the coffins,
eat breadcrumb and marrow and declare your nation in Cyrillic.
Follow the dopplering of the motorcade, trace the path
of your soused shadow toward an uncertain star
in the middle distance that burns through sleep
against a terracotta dome, against a tower some Cosimo
watches anxiously to execute the hour's newly minted curse.

12.

If there's a form inside a thing, like a human
shape inside a rock, then there's a miracle
of balance inside a drunk on a bicycle
navigating the streets of the brain—
maybe he just cannot lose. Congressmen
leech mutability like phosphorous
into the flickering crowd
almost knocking the king from his seat
atop a contraption of wire and steel
some fool sketched in a notebook
so this huffing dervish could go forth
to raise his flag of money
where the pandemonium of history
refuses to die on a chalk-silhouette street.
We are composed of newspaper, rag, cigarette butts,
emulsifiers, wool, and a gold florin.
Some prince's man watched a drunkard
on a horse once and invented the cantilevered
arm. That is how we abandon nature for art—
not to praise some god who remains aloof,
but to hail the King, to worship the thing burning
inside him like Dionysius' ruby bead: our crimson flail.

13.

Grief brings the minstrel to the old city
where corporate towers were built in stone
that only dreamed of plastic and strontium,
where the first corporate engines ate a fuel
of dye and blood and minted nickel reveries—
O lost home between fields and citadel,
O fatal renaissance, fevered dream,
O pool of demons who rise and flood furies
through my mind to drown the child inside,
some poor Lorenzo or Lincoln swept up
by memory's distortion of time's waters,
some Roosevelt a duke smiled to scorn
while still holding my slender slats of rib
to peer out at his future: a crowd
weighed down with purses and bags who step
on stilts like herons poised to stab at minnows.
I cycle against the tide, the throng, the groundlings
under the loggia. I ride through all these selves
staring into their hands as they go.
I sing and try to rise above the swirling radionuclides
but falling fail, drown and drop, orphean.
The underworld has many windows
open to the narcotic of widowed night.
The present moment is an ancient place.
It rises in towers above our towns,
above this you, above this me, above the shore
where Pluto fills his digital well to baffle
a revenant . . . . even a drunkard knows the length
of his hand. We ride somnambulant, a trinket
on a mobile's scale, a clown rowing a Napoleon
hat through a madman's blueprint of the near future
or recent past, a balancing suspense that cannot last
like wind from the east, as if time had seen its ghost.
Poor Tom. Peace, Smulkin. The violets wither.

14.

Witness: when the drunken man rides his bicycle
through the piazza, we recoil and advance
like mice at the mercy of his whims: now he bumps
the fruit vendor, now he glances off the window
at the bank, now he knocks over the woman
with sacks of groceries—passersby catch the oranges
and apples and bottles but the drunkard he lifts
his hand in triumph: what dexterity, what balance,

what a man! A taxi smashes into the pharmacy
to avoid the wheeling bike, the man on the church
steps flinches as more broadcast groceries arc
toward him in a trajectory of circus colors.
The scene unfolds with logic and necessity,
and however reluctant we may be
to devote ourselves to him, a part of us gives it up
for the randomness of what he'll do next,
for the careening of the wheels, for the tossed
curse and catcalls as he lifts his legs
into the shape of a nun's wimple athwart the frame,
balance askew, final catastrophe now certain.
And it is like both the strophe and antistrophe
of old tragedy and the child whose antics
dominate the room. Caution and concern
become the edge of their own cutting blade
as a virtual somersault, like the inebriate tumbling
over cartoon cobblestones in a cartoon fit,
spills pedestrian blood like graffiti against the walls.

15.

On the stage it's a monkey riding a bicycle,
but in the world beyond the mind, balloons
are bombs, antics and hijinks are carnage
and war, feint and bluff are rebar
and white hoods. On the stage the tyrant is a toy,
in the world, murder. A simple sneer
and a whole people maligned, a gesture
of self-promotion, sleeves shot at the expense
of an entire race, a swerve, a honking of the toy
horn, a clown flares smilingly, the monkey primping,
stoking the furnace of self idolatry, stroking the tiny
member with a grin. Too, the nation's monkey
mind, barbarous and trivial, flickers
in the imagination of continents, a smirk flashes
over the mirrors of self and the illusions multiply
in the lurid light of the baboons' crimson asses' glow.
The audience is gullible, sincere, naïve, trembling,
half in love with the wag. Then the network spills
its headline: Jesus must have been a hater too, love
his lash and whip. Blessed are the righteous,
for they will vanquish the losers. We retreat
to the altar of television and screen, for sex
and bedtime stories in thrall of the monkey
and his coined wilderness. See the cigarette
in the adorable grip of the baby chimp, see

a thousand fires smoldering in the nation's upholstery.
Each crimson coal bores a hole through eternity
to the underworld of dreams, anorectic
and chemical, drowned in the pupil-blackened
hatches tattooed against the believers' scored palms.
Violent night, holy night.

16.

Surely we've come to the end of something,
the end of the same thing we thought we saw die
when B-52s climbed the whirligigs of jungle
trees and shut their eyes against the napalm,
when drenched sands redeployed the groans
with pit-bulls and the hard-wired genitals
of the enemy were renditioned in old palace walls.
Were we bankrupt all along, those false hopes
we called enlightenment and renaissance
dying all these years from heartworm wheedling
doubt into sawdust however much we wished
to have, along the battlements, the muffled darkness
unfold to reveal some origin or answer, either right
or wrong? Surely we have travelled here
to see some tangle of hope and despair loosened
at a border crossing under shade of a mesquite,
only to find a wounded king fishing in the mud,
a sick queen disguised as a beggar to undo
desire or desire's obliteration—surely we have
travelled here to find something that will make us
feel whole again, or purposefully broken,
a code switch obscure scribes predicted
on a master stone a dead age scored and read
eons ago that will make us say this is our us:
this is what and what for, this the room,
this the bed, this the door that leads to a door,
this the word that found a home on our tongue
before it died in our ears, before it turned to ash,
this the gorgon face tattooed on the wall
of an inconsequential heart. And now a monkey
riding a scooter on a horse's back—maybe it's you,
maybe it's me who wears an impresario's top hat,
ringmaster whip in hand to beat down the humanity.
Sleep, Nuncle, sleep. Poor Tom will make him
weep and wail, his horn is dry. They will lay him
in the cold ground, at his heels a stone.
Pansies for thoughts.

17.

A clown serving plums to a voracious queen:
we know enough to know this is how it begins,
crumbs of words sprinkled across the dark
pool that opens inside an ego's screen. Furies
clamber up ribs, their faces surfacing like fish
taking shapes of desire that never died. And now
they morph and molt, swell and worm,
shed and ming from the atoms of the broken
centuries. This is what the old debris do
in fertile earth: seek and find their way to light,
the tubers half rotten, half green with rot,
ancient hatreds, buried jealousies. The end of peace
begins with war, roots of blood stirring
in new dirt. A monstrous imagination
gestates, disseminates fire and blood,
seeks purchase in the soil of the angry class.
Must all the monsters we slay wear our own faces?
(The child within slew me with just this sword
to cut the old man's ravings: rosemary, rue).

18.

We need a Medusa at this end of things,
a head of hair composed of snakes.
We need to cut out a heart and eat it
in the marketplace of this America,
we need to hold up Perseus' head
as the emblem of the new gorgon
the colonizer of minds, weaver of illusions—
O Child: decipher the aged stains
we read as prophecy growing up
from age's dregs in childhood's cup.

19.

America grows old. Mesmerized, scripted
on a screen, we watch the man on the bicycle
careen in antic shapes of a clown, a wind-up
toy or grainy cartoon with a wobbly music
of Betty-Boop or Popeye, saint or Madonna
in a black and white film or school-kid doodles
in a tablet turned flip-book—look at the man
who holds his brain like a flute of rare vintage
precarious over the cobblestones, look at his dog,

Little John, race ahead in a dream of rut
through the ancient arcades.
Look at the pantomime desire apes
aping desire, a monkey on a tin horse,
calavera on a cattail reed:
Step up right this way!—watch a man
turn into a spume of dust, watch a nation
crumble into a spatter of zinc and neurotoxins.
Behold the drunken man on the bicycle
veering over the flagstones of history,
smashing monuments like stale cookies
groping the perfumed bodies pressed
against a wall. . . . listen to the laughter
of the crowd . . . . there's a mouth on a drunken
bicycle floating on a blue ocean,
a voice whose wheels ride on currents
from his own lungs, the thermals his voice
amplifies in his cave and in the world
rising now as, airborne, he teeters toward
you and toward me, toward the opiate
oblivion of a trinket vendor's stall.

20.

Our faces are trinkets in a vendor's stall,
ears are nests a crow's lust for glitter
has feathered with silver.
The King colonizes the weak places.
A fontanel erodes under weather
of a radio voice. A god worms
the apple where the vulnerable
flesh of fruit has built its private
sweetness. The whine of a blood angel
tells history how it must unfold,
how flesh will become juice,
how the self will be deployed
in wars as the host cheers for madness,
as the nation thrills to be a toy
in the hands of a drunken man,
a bauble to juggle, words as toys
in the teeth of the drunken man,
whose medieval locomotions assemble
civic order of catapult and wagon.
Not me, not you, but hailed
as the only purity,
the one wild card,
infused with his own blood,

flush with chemicals and courage.
American, the original word,
the only beginning,
the only brave word.

21.

Hog in sloth,
fox in stealth,
dog in madness.
Come, unbutton here.
Maybe it was only
a small coin,
to have been so easily
given away,
our America.
We must wear
our rue
with a difference,
savor
the world's eating.

22.

Somewhere beyond the reach
of nation we remember voices
outside the window
beyond the hedge,
maybe you, maybe me,
sunlight and headlights
shifting across a wall,
plastic men in cinderblock
puddles, all bright as colors:
cars, flavors, sounds.
Somewhere beyond
the reach of nation you and I
remember the animal
building its nest in the shadow
of a well where
a traveler stops for water.
Somewhere beyond
the wrenching
and the howls,
drink, Traveler,
and be confused again.

23.

A canvas tent folds into steel and air
and Monkey sleeps on the neck
of a horse. Baboon murmurs
against the solar plexus
of the contortionist.
The world fills with smoke
and lavender.
Pilgrims begin a road
paralytics and lepers limped
in darkness.
The kilns forge gorgon masks.
Fragments. Sparks.
Houses of paper shift in wind.

WITH APOLOGIES TO ANTON CHEKHOV

by Julie Stielstra

Semyon Grigorevich was feeling unusually tired. He had almost quarrelled with his fiancée the evening before, and went home early to bed. He slept badly, and his breakfast sausage roll was like felt in his mouth.

He went to see Dr. Chekhov. The doctor placed one end of a wooden tube in his own ear, and pressed the bell at the other end against Semyon Grigorevich's breastbone, then his back, then his chest again.

"Well," said Dr. Chekhov, "your heart is working too hard. It may be a valve that is leaking."

Semyon Grigorevich sat back in his chair. "What does that mean? Am I going to die? Soon? Or slowly? What should I do?"

Dr. Chekhov drummed his fingers on the desktop. "You must take good care of yourself. You must not overexert yourself, eat rich meals, smoke, or drink. You must rest and get plenty of sleep every night, and not get overexcited. With that regimen, you may be quite comfortable for many years. Come back in three months and we'll see how you're faring."

That evening, over a basin of plain broth and a glass of tea, Semyon Grigorevich pondered those months—and years. No more dancing. No more wine. No more leisurely pipes of tobacco by the fire, getting worked up over politics with his friends late into the night, and... The next day, he released Maria Alexandrovna from their engagement. She cried a little, but not too much, so he was able to avoid becoming too distressed. He slept better that night.

Semyon Grigorevich became a student of his health. He took his temperature each morning and each evening. He checked his pulse several times a day, and if it exceeded 85 beats per minute (he counted out a full minute by his watch), he stopped what he was doing and would lie down until it returned to 75. He kept a detailed diary of these measurements, which included his activities, his food, and the frequency and condition of his bowels. It pleased him when he could correlate these things, and he scrupulously eliminated any food suspected of association with fluctuations in the observations. Within a few weeks, he had established a firm menu of water, tea, gruel, boiled vegetables, porridge without milk or sugar, plain bread (a few drops of honey were permitted on Saturdays), and lightly steamed fish (also on Saturdays).

He lost weight. And, once all the rules and schedules and observations were in train, he became a bit bored. And lonely.

There was a café in the town, a few streets from his house. He had determined that a gentle walk of no more than fifteen minutes, three times a day, did not disturb his equilibrium. It was a pleasant summer day, so the air would not harm him. Three men sat outside this café (he had noticed them before), sharing a bench, each with his own tea or cordial before him. Semyon Grigorevich decided to sit down and have a glass of tea as well. He nodded in a friendly way to the men, and they nodded back.

The man at the end of the bench, where the sun shone full upon him, was thin and very pale, though his cheeks were flushed. He often coughed, pressing a handkerchief to his mouth. The man next to him was much older, stooped and stiff, his gnarled hands locked around the handle of a walking stick. He sat on a structure of cushions, to pad his hips and back, and he had a pouch at his feet to carry the cushions in. The third man, who sat at the shadiest end of the bench, was sallow and very thin indeed. He sipped often at a footed cup into which he dissolved packets of powder.

"Does that new medicine help you much?" the coughing man asked the thin man.

The thin man answered, "I'm not sure. I've only been taking it for a week, and I was up with terrible griping in my belly three times last night."

Semyon Grigorevch began to listen with interest.

"That happened to me," said the stiff, crooked man. "Only it turned out to be the medicine itself that caused it."

"Sometimes," said the coughing man, "I'm glad there is no medicine for me. Just rest and air and sunshine, they said. I can't afford to go to one of those sanitariums in the mountains."

Politely, Semyon Grigorevich asked the coughing man: "Is there any diet prescribed for you? I've developed a little cough, and syrup of honey and lemon has soothed that. It isn't unpleasant."

The coughing man laughed. "Honey and lemon is no good for what I have!"

"He's consumptive," the crooked man told Semyon Grigorevich. The coughing man shrugged and smiled with some pride. "That's why we let him sit in the sunniest spot. Though sometimes he lets me sit there. It feels good on these rheumatic old bones of mine, and he's very fair about it."

"My doctor says I need to follow a strict diet," said Semyon Grigorevich. "I think it may be helping, but I have to obey it to the letter."

"What does he recommend?" asked the very thin man. "What does your doctor say is wrong with you? Who do you see?"

"Dr. Chekhov says it is my heart," announced Semyon Grigorevich. The three men nodded gravely, listening intently. Semyon Grigorevich explained his regimen and his measurements.

"Chekhov is good," said the very thin man. "But he's not a bowel man. I have an ulcerated bowel, and he could do nothing for me. You're lucky, you're not in pain like I am."

"Yes, but it's his heart," said the arthritic man. "That's much more worrisome. I've heard a bad heart can cause a cough."

"Yes, but many things can cause a cough," said the consumptive man. And he would know, thought Semyon Grigorevich.

And so they whiled away an hour or two, sitting in the sun, sipping their drinks. The ulcerated bowel man promised to bring Semyon Grigorevich a recipe for a nourishing soup that was good for the blood, and in exchange, Semyon Grigorovich told him how he made his porridge, which was very bland and might not irritate his tender internal tissues. The arthritic man didn't say very much after that, and Semyon Grigorevich wondered if he resented him, as a newcomer, with his more interesting and dangerous illness.

But after that, they met often. "That ticker still ticking?" the arthritic man would greet him jovially. The ulcerated bowel man thanked Semyon Grigorevich for the porridge instructions, and said he would add it to his menu. Semyon Grigorevich showed his notebooks to the consumptive man, who was impressed and began to make his own notes more regularly. He also advised Semyon Grigorevich when he found he was getting short of breath climbing the stairs or if he walked too quickly, and taught him some breathing exercises to practice.

At the end of the summer, when three months had passed, Semyon Gregorovich returned to Dr. Chekhov's office. The doctor listened to his chest again and shrugged. "About the same, I think," he said. "How are you feeling?"

Semyon Grigorovich sighed. "Not better," he said. "I've done everything you said, but I'm still tired, and now I get a little breathless sometimes, and have to slow down."

"Then I think you must consider going to see Dr. Braunwald in the city. He's a specialist in disorders of the heart. If there's something wrong there, he can tell you. I'll write him and tell him you'll come to see him."

Semyon Grigorevich felt rather dejected when he got on the train to the city. His friends at the café had wished him well and encouraged him, but he was beginning to wonder if he would ever feel better.

Dr. Braunwald was a big, ruddy, hearty man who looked as though he had never been ill in his life. "So, let's have a listen, shall we?" he said cheerily. He had a fancier tool than Dr. Chekhov did: two rubber tubes with little ear pieces fitted into each ear, and the metal bell was pressed to Semyon Grigorevich's sternum. The doctor listened for a long time. He moved the bell to different places on the chest, along his spine, against his ribs, and back to the chest, asking Semyon Grigorevich to breathe in and out at different times. He felt the pulses in Semyon Grigorevich's throat, in his wrists, even in his feet and, gently, in the crease of his groin. Then he sat back, smiling.

"Semyon Grigorevich, there is nothing whatever wrong with your heart. It beats strongly, regularly, with no leaking or rubbing or murmur-

By midnight, he was curled up in a tight ball in his bed. His belly churned and growled; his head throbbed. Oh, he had done too much! Too much, too quickly! His pulse was racing. He sat by the open window to cool his damp forehead. Could Dr. Braunwald have been mistaken? But he was the specialist! The expert! It was his own fault. He had to be more careful.

ing. Your pulses are steady and strong. You're a bit pale, and you say you've lost weight. I would tell you to go out to a nice restaurant, order yourself a good piece of beef with noodles and mushroom sauce, and a glass or two of good red wine. Have some dessert! Go home. Get plenty of fresh air and exercise. Enjoy life. You have nothing to fear from your heart."

Rather stunned, Semyon Gregorovich did what he was told. The steak was thick and juicy and utterly delicious. The wine slipped sweetly down. He ate a large apple tart with cream, and then dared to smoke one small cigar. He couldn't wait to get home and tell his friends at the café.

He felt better in the morning. He ate just a small piece of toast, as his poached egg looked too rich, too yellow and bright. He shuffled up and down in the street, but had to go back inside to lie down when his heart begin to thump. By now, he didn't even need to count it, he could just feel when it was too fast. His joy had turned into fear. It would be up to him alone now, not to ruin everything.

Late in the afternoon, he crept timidly to the café.

"You're back!" cried the arthritic man.

"What did the heart specialist say?" asked the consumptive man eagerly.

The ulcerated bowel man gulped his cordial and asked, "How are you feeling now?"

Semyon Grigorevich took a deep breath. "He said…" he began haltingly, "…he told me there is nothing wrong with my heart at all!"

His friends were astonished.

"Why, that's wonderful!"

"What excellent news!"

"You must be delighted!"

After a moment, Semyon Grigorevich said, "Yes, I suppose. But…"

"But what?" they all three cried.

"But I don't feel any better than before."

"But you've been told there's nothing wrong with you," said the consumptive man irritably. "I wish someone could tell *me* that."

The arthritic man held up his hand, whose warped fingers he could barely move. "No doubts about what's wrong with me. Anyone can see it."

The ulcerated bowel man suddenly got up, hurried inside, and was inside for some time. When he finally returned, he said only, "I have to go home now." And left.

"Sometimes he gets attacks like that," said the consumptive man. "It's very painful for him."

No one said anything for some time.

"Well," said the consumptive man. "It's very good news for you. I hope you'll feel better very soon."

"Unlike some of us," said the arthritic man.

Semyon Grigorevich walked slowly home. He couldn't finish his steamed fish, and went to bed early after drinking a glass of warmed water with ginger. If he was very careful, he might end up being all right. But who would he tell?

THE OWLET AND THE TURTLE
by Greg Sendi
_____

Come up into my nesty bed,
the Owlet to the Turtle said.

Here will I feed you nuts and mice,
here cosset you in wings and twice

each day, at sunrise and at gloam,
lay kisses dewed with honeycomb

and stainy crush of thicket grape
upon your ancient leathery nape.

Here talon you behind the ears,
here hold your riddles years and years,

and guerdon you with balmy myrtle,
so fiercely do I love you, Turtle.

Together we may bless a nesty bed
the Owlet to her darling Turtle said.

In fervid yawp to roost above
rejoined the Turtle to his love:

Dear treasured caller, windfall Owl,
here overhear my rapt avowal

receive from quaggy mat below
my moon-rinsed consort song and know

but for your feathery sylvan art
(beloved, gaze in your own heart!)

no rest might mend the blemishes
that cram these shell-hulled premises,

no other soul my secrets keep.
Thus, straining as he might to leap

in turtle vaults toward the roost above,
rejoined the Turtle to his Owlet love.

SYLVANUS, BARD

by Marc Lerner

In the nineteenth chapter of Gibbon's *Decline and Fall* we read the astonishing and melancholy story of Sylvanus, a Roman general in the provinces of Gaul under the reign of Constantius. The court of that emperor was controlled by a corrupt and scheming cabal of eunuchs and ministers, who conspired to forge some letters of the hitherto entirely loyal Sylvanus' to give the appearance that he planned to attempt a *coup*. The immediate danger to his person prompted Sylvanus to attempt the very thing he was unjustly charged with, and he assumed the purple at Cologne, only to be assassinated after a reign of twenty-eight days.

The idea of a false accusation leading to the performance of the same act of which one is accused seems almost preternaturally pregnant with theatrical possibilities. One can easily imagine a play of Shakespeare's with this narrative; Sylvanus would begin with devotion towards the emperor perhaps stronger even than that of Brutus, and in his dying moments reflect that his sincere wish to serve Constantius with fealty was subverted by the inhuman exigencies of Fate.

The element of fatalism inherent in Shakespeare's tragedies is, of course, an enervated one compared to the rigorous determinism we find in other, older, cultures. In the *Bhagavad Gita*, the prince Arjuna is hesitant to fight a war in which he finds many of his family members and friends on the opposing side. Krishna exhorts him to this task by pointing out that his enemies in battle "have already been slain by me: tremble not, fight and slay them" (11.34). If a writer with this kind of worldview took up the task of writing a play about Sylvanus, the actions of the treacherous ministers and eunuchs would likely themselves be the direct result of divine intervention – perhaps a demonstration of the deity's ability to influence events to any end, despite the loyal general's unwillingness to rebel. Such celestial interference in human affairs reminds us also of Homer, whose treatment of the story would likely have also been of this nature.

Modern life, of course, tends rather in the opposite direction to this; in the West, at the least, we are oppressed by the problems of too much moral freedom, rather than not enough. If a Camus, for example, took on the task of writing about Sylvanus (as he did, in fact, about Caligula), one suspects that the general's dying reflections would be presented with a knowing and resigned smile, acknowledging that the roles of loyal subject and usurper were one and the same and both subsumed in the absurdity of human life. Stepping from the twentieth century to the dregs of the twenty-first, we might also speculate about the artificially depressed faux-conservative Michel Houellebecq (presuming, of course, that he could produce something featuring a main character that was not just a variant of himself). His Sylvanus would likely proclaim with a malicious and maudlin nihilism that he preferred the degenerated state in which he ended his existence, and that everyone else's life would be the same.

This last example, whilst of an inferior quality from a literary standpoint, is an instructive one psychologically. It is obvious that what we have in Houellebecq is a man who has *chosen to hate his life*, and whilst it is natural to think of all these writers that their own characters and beliefs would influence their interpretation of the Sylvanus story, everyone knows that the behaviour of people like Houellebecq is self-reinforcing: the more self-pitying books he writes, the more like the books he becomes. In truth, the most salient causality flows in reverse to the natural one: how we do our work becomes who we are, and as assuredly as the child is the father of the man, Sylvanus is the father of the bard. Writing an abstracted analysis in place of a play is, of course, an expression of this same causality.

ROT AND GLORIANA

by Laurel Miram

This revelation was born at the intersection of two grocery aisles, though it might have dawned anywhere and everything would have followed on in the same way.

I am typically cautious with shopping carts at aisle turns, but like all creatures I harden under sedimentary pressures on occasion, in the depths of which self-preservation proves antonymic, and at such times veering toward a crossroads—*any* crossroads—is worth the hazard for the chance at air it brings.

So it was (and thus was I) on the verge of her emergence. Rattled and preoccupied, yearning for home and an hour's ease, I hurtled toward the end of the aisle, the end of the list, the end of pleading ends. Recklessness plays at freedom and so did I. But nature abhors a forged abandon, and my affected rush fell desolate, impotent.[1] An *imminence* mounted between my end and me. It halted my propulsion, tried to prepare me. It would have been reprehensible to launch into the space she was about to inhabit. I heeded a foreign instinct to wait upon the unknown.

Life is a series of forgettable encounters. Remembrance is a pledge, a contract of the mind. Signatures are required to bring memory to the table and make it commit. It craves impasto and gestalt. Slant. Flourish.

I reared as she ushered herself into view.[2] Here was a walking life frame. A grave, stolid skeleton who shifted past before me, eclipsing my presence, enlisting my future.

But slowly, so slowly, each step a conservation. I cannot say she shuffled; that would be unjust. She deliberated with her paces, as one who has had to learn how. She picked them up and carried them in arms cinched taut about her body, two ends of the same twine, holding the whole back from collapse like ribbon coiled around gift wrap when the tape's run out.

And that was her regalia. There was no hint of the sufferer about her, no cry of sickly or aged indignation, no breath of loss. It might have been acceptance, or perhaps its mortal enemy, or some odd commingling even she did not understand, but somehow this woman, this fastidiously kempt tower of jarring angularity beneath barely worn, perfectly pressed blue and white, minced footfalls as if they were of no consequence and all consequence, as if they were the proper rate of change, as if none more able than she could be found in the entirety of the building.[3]

There's nothing left of her, I thought without thinking, for I had not her wisdom. *Is it cancer? Old age? Something broken, or incurable? What toll, what cost to make her way around, to take this walk about the store?*

Her rebuke was unspoken. Certainly unaware. Equally as convicting as her arrival.

I know how I appear, she said. *I scale toil and cost and I daily count currency. I keep my accounts as I do my hair, my clothes. Beyond interest in what I have left, or what is owing, or what has been denied, I am here, I am walking. I will still be walking when you remember me in the evening, swallowing footprints, afraid to meet my slightest stride. I will walk out of this skin in glory. What will you?*

And so she walks, wending through my shame like a time snake—the kind that wraps you up when escape's run out—slowly, so slowly, balancing, reckoning, weighing the cost of air against columns I've left to rot, waiting for Gloriana.

---

1 That is the way of things with human creatures; we are alone amongst the living in this respect. The petal, the seed, the bested lion and postpartum octopus, the queen's indeterminate mate: do they not give themselves to dissolution without regard? Who among us is so blind with knowing, so dangerously capable of release?

2 My shopping cart might have indulged me and lifted its front wheels to oblige my metaphor. It did not, but now I have insinuated the image anyway, so for the purposes of this reading, it did.

3 I suspect she holds this truth self-evident, wherever she goes.

LEARNING TO WALK

by Jodie Dalgleish

———————————

I watch your boots press their downwards force into the dirt,
and its deep forest litter. I see their compression of it;
how a heel strikes the distinct trace of your weight, in humus,
and how it rebounds, as if decomposing upwards, our long
hard-pressed relations coming back on up, to the arch
as the heft of the body moves itself, onto its toes,
from the great toe, to the second, to the third, and so on:
the body's lift, to the 'toe-off,' and the load of the 'stance
phase' of the gait to be perambulated over ground. How the
valley has loft itself into the strata of schistose rock—time
in foliated, metamorphic rock, up-ended into its mineral
sheaths, sheared along our escarpment: the grand cuts
of orange sericite, green ottrelite, and the sandstone that
has been veined in quartzite, coming up tight and tipped
to the course of our feet. How the heel lifts and is swung
by the foot, in a pendulum, from the hip, to the plant
of the reciprocal leg's pendular pivot; it's like pole-vaulting
off one reiterative stake to the next while the rolling torque
of each hip couples the fall of an arc with the rise of an arc:
how our centre is carried undulately in the constantly, re-
directional, work of our 'step-to-step transitions.' How the
lungs fill to the signals of the receptors in our blood, telling us
how deeply we need to breathe with effort, in the swell
of the belly: sensors at the arterial bifurcation of the throat,
and on the heart's aortic arch, rounding our abdomens out
to the thoracic cavity's influx of air. Where there's a view
from the top of our rock-range spur, out over the land's hook
of the river; its meander that rings us, always, into the setting
of its alluvial settling—our hands out, over the rail,
evidencing the way all the ridges arrow their way into that
boucle and its almost-island of stone-housed tracts of land.
Stood with the last details of the valley's walls, it's the 'light touch
contact' of the index finger that will take us back down, trailing
through bracken, and heather: that slight 'shear force' at the
tip of the 'tactile stimulations of the hand', that's enough
to maintain 'postural control,' to keep our bodies' 'equilibrate sway'
in play. There's how rhizomatous bracken succeeded the first
forest ferns and how the perennial of heather (perhaps) branched
from its seeded ones and flowered the first woodlands from which
angiosperms then bloomed; how a bracken fern's apical blade ('frond')
has unfurled its 'crozier' (tip) and is, fractally, 'tri-pinnate'—from the 'rachis'
(stem) of the blade to the 'pinna', pinna to 'pinnule', pinnule to 'pinnulet';
with 'sori' that trace the lobed divisions of each subleaflet's margins.

Saying, how heather extends apically too, in branches of leading long shoots
that branch into short shoots, and leading long shoots that branch into both
short shoots and leading long shoots, making the 'hemispherical' shrub
with its concentrically radial flower—criss-crossed from two whorls
of leaf bracts to one darker, mauve, petal-like 'calyx', to the inside lighter, pink,
'corolla' of the 'perianth' (the outer part of the 'flower'); how, in a cross-section,
we'd see the way its particular nectary sits down below the 'fruiting' bulb to
sequester the bell-like corolla of the sequential flower. How the shrub enters
dormancy with clusters of (end-of-season) short shoots that break to long-
leading flowering shoots, and previous, surviving, long shoots might bloom
progressively, downwards; back from the waymarked rim of the *'Roche à
Sept Heures'* where, at 7 AM in the morning, the sun hits the end of our
escarpment, tossing out the *éclairant* quartz-rich siliceous rock, in a
vitreous éclat of the valley's crystal: scene of its trailed surface struck
out slab-like; light salvo, under our feet.

**Variation of original published in Shearsman *125 & 126, Winter 2020/2021.*

MAP OF MEMORY

by Jesse Schotter

A voice. Calling to wake me out of sleep. Asking me to think of a thing I have forgotten. Of a sigh of a man who is cursed for a burden, the cry of a woman for her child that is lost. Is it the wind whispering? Shouts of the shopmen, words blurred? From dreams drowning the morning drags me up. To hear the citysounds again, cartwheel moan and the snuff of gaslights. Noiseblend from the sootstreets, to coil in my ears.

Eyes closed. The lightspecks of dreamsleep still flashing in the darkness. What is it, the word? To my mudheavy tongue it does not come. In a language that is not mine. *Glivorem*: Fireflies. Yes. The rain or earth or what lit them blew them to birth. From the grass and grain and the cool stream rising, back in Volapzhin where the road to Kiev curved. In the oncoming nights, when I was beautiful. Floating in fullness past the foolboys watching.

Thirty-five years or more ago. Before the journey to this America, the deaths and might-as-well-be deaths. Such a span of time and yet still I remember. The waterlight coming clean over the roofs at dayend. To wash the roads like rain. The sun thronesitting at the streamedge, winking Godeye picking out in light the high tree leaves. You, you, I choose, not you. In the mudstreets the broken pots and chicken blood turned to gold dust and our house to polished brass, warm flameedge orange. Light burning blinding and my eyes from the synagogue the shops dazzled away. Our faces glowing beautiful, mama's and papa's and mine.

Misha with his rough tongue begging for scraps and the streetdogs feeling in their fur the dusk coming. Shh, the day said, like mama in her moods, shhh!, and the noises hushed. The light

still strong in the high clouds but down here darkening quick to night. The world sent like a child early to bed and the parents in the daysky talking loud. And then the sun dropped down and the pink clouds faded, in the east still tipped with orange but blackening quickly west to darker deep blue winter blue. The knit of light loosening, and the stores and houses, the Dubinsky's and the Abramson's and the Pevzner's, dissolving to dull grey brown. Wood boards blending and the deep ruts smoothed. Streethouses pressed flat like flowers in mama's book, dark rectangles and squares and then fading. Screen after screen of night dropping, blotting like Herschel's ink. Gone the synagogue at the roadbend, grainfields distant, weeds on the streetedge. All cleaned in the pure darkness.

The black nightwall close now; only the porch left behind in the grayness. And then as if breathed up from groundfire the fireflies would rise. Mama said watch and I watched close and they winked at me and I waited again for them to wink *Wink!* but each time different and I did not know where they would come again or when. Before only darkness and papa's snores but now in pinholes of light I could see the roadmud and the house across the way where Basia lived. The trees there once more for a moment in the green circles and the grass green in pieces. For hours they danced, the fireflies, rising and falling in and out like breath but no pattern.

But eyes open. Into black oceanwater Volapzhin sinks, up over housetops and spires and gone. The fireflies quenched in the darkness, green lidblots dissolving. Of a beautiful dream there is no use, if the dawn in the room is cold. Clay pots on the dustshelves, dull rugpatterns twined. A gasp of breath: mine. Jacob beside me with his snores. The whereplace returning. New York, New World. 5673. 1913. The 21st of May. Oil lamps shining warm gold, but no fireflies.

It is too much of a muchness, too soon in the morning. A rumble deep in my head. Hoofbeats? Fistgrasp at my breath. The burnflush rising. But it is only little Avrom, mouth open stirring in the cradle. The street outside is calm, buildings unburnt. No high whinny of horses, crack of hoof on wood before the splintering. I rise from the bed, feel the rough ridges of the planks against my footsoles. My eyes can see in the darkness: the stove, the cradle. In Avrom's ear I whisper soft in English. His legs fat like his father's kicking against the night. He will know more than me, more than Lea, new language and old stories too. But English is hard, a glove that does not fit. Always another finger outsticking, no cloth to cover. And dreams the hardest; at night the books the signs in Volapzhin still in Yiddish or in Kiev "ні євреї."

Still three hours till the dawn, but a change in the thickness of darkness. Enough to see the patterns of the wallpaper, the wood table with faded brown cloth, marked by the old lines of Lea's school ink.

A flash of white on the pocked woodfloor. Reflecting for a moment the moonlight. A square of paper, half-tucked beneath the apartment door. It has been slid there, in the night. I stoop to look. Left top corner crumpled, greyed by dust. It is a knife: to cut my breast with its edges. Telling me I am not safe. Notes can be slipped in secret to me: threats. Robbers can scale the buildingsides and pry back the windowframes. This room is nothing. I press my hand to the door. Strong and solid it seems, but it is like the curtain walls at the theaters, letting through light and anything. Who else will come with their words to wound me?

But it is from Lea. I know already. I unfold the creases of the paper. Scrawled inside is her child writing: the looping g's and unsteady d's. *I am coming to see you tonight. It will be good for us to talk.*

I am the you she is coming to see. Not Jacob, still asleep. Did she drop the letter off with Mrs. Teplitsky? Or in the silent hours of night creep up the stairs to place it here herself? I press myself to my feet, my knees aching. Always now I can feel my bones and body that before were light and nothing.

I watch Jacob, his chest swelling like sea waves before the break, swaddled in the red and purple coverlet. He knows of this. They have met in secret. Planned it all. Conspiring against me.

America has made them weak. Lea has learnt nothing. At her age I had lived two lives for her one. Soaring I had come in birdflight across miles

and countries, plains of Kiev to the valleys of Wall Street. A continent and an ocean. In horse-cart and steerage. She does not know hunger, like I know. She does not know the struggles and the sufferings, or the happinesses that were. And so she did not listen. Meeting with the nogood men after the sweatshop sewing that I had not wanted for her to do. Already I had begun to suspect: that little fatness around her middle. "What have you been eating?" I asked. "The look of you—it is a power you should not lose."

It was over dinner; cabbage and kasha. "I am pregnant," she blurted, her elbow striking the tableside hard.

Jacob blinking as if it waved the fact away. "What?" he cried. "You are to be married?" The innocent.

She pouted, face red and angry behind the tears. "He has run off."

"The swine!" Jacob cried.

"And you did this with him?" I asked. "One of these American shysters you love so much? On about his money and his plans, 'you are more beautiful than the Gentile girls'?"

"No, mama. It was not like that. He was …"

"I do not want to hear of this filth. You are a shanda."

"Minna…" Jacob's hand on my shoulder, trying to stop my feelings, as he always does.

Lea's face was blank. Dead.

"Go, go," I said. "I am used to this. You will leave me anyway. It may as well be now."

The fire was bright in my eyes and my breath short. But the words were not quite right to say what I wanted.

"I don't understand," Jacob said to me, his face open in appeal. "She is not asking to leave."

But she had thrown away what we have given her. For Jacob in Volapzhin said, "we want a better place for our children. We must go to the New World." So: the town gone and mama and the horse heaving its dying sighs and Jacob choking down his shame. For what? Her future now is only shame and the squalidness of the sweat-shoppers we had almost worked ourselves free of. And if so then why have we endured the horrors of this world and the passage here?

"I don't know what you want of me," Lea whispered. "I don't know what you want." Like an old woman she stood from the table, unsteady.

I want this world to be Volapzhin. I want Lea to be a success but not in the ways of this America. I want the time then to be the time now. These things that are not possible.

"Out of my house, whore," I cried. Unfaithful to my care for her.

She swayed like a tree beaten by the wind. "What? Where will I live?" She looked at me with the face of a child forced to see sights too much for her. A face I know well. And then as if shocked from the subway rails she bolted down the stairs. A silence as of breath being held and Jacob running after her, coming back with eyes like holes waiting to be filled. But he is a coward and went along.

So then a return eight months later and her bastard child forced on me. She will not stay again beneath this roof, but for Avrom who cries in the night I have relented. Now I am stuck to go through it again with this lump of flesh that wants and wants when it was done and over.

Still Jacob does not accept. Asking yesterday again, "Why is it that you will not welcome her?" He is always asking why. Wanting to talk and wonder. "It is not her getting together with the boy, is it?" he said. "Because we did too before the wedding, you remember. So, she is unlucky with the child. She has paid, she is sorry. A mitzveh it is, to be blessed with a family. It is too much for you at your age to care for a newborn."

"What age is that?"

"We too can be blessed." Ignoring as always.

"She is no longer my daughter," I said.

He shrugged his hands up, breath out hot. "Why? Why this still? It is two months now that we have had Avrom, eleven months without Lea, the fruit of our souls. Is not that too long? We must take her back."

But I sat silent. While our love was strong we lay on the edge of a sword, now a couch sixty yards wide is too narrow for us. He with his talking, over and over again, plowing the land that has been plowed. Talk is worth a dollar; silence is worth two. For why should I say or

know why I feel? The same with the sadnesses that creep on me. I could say, "It is the days with nothing to do, only to sew, no books to read," but now with teaching there is something in the days and I have the library to visit for the books. And still the sadnesses. Jacob before would sit beside me and ask, "What is wrong, my *kinigl?*" but I had no want to talk or to explain. It is as if they require happiness of us. To sing of this land, this America. This America that takes my daughter and my past. She eats the seeds of the fruit of this world until she is ruined for anywhere but here. Distracted by the clothes on the mannequins in the store windows and not seeing the blankness of their faces and their hands cut off.

I tell a story that no one in this New World wants for me to tell. For how can we sing songs in a world that is strange? To my mouth's roof my tongue cleaves.

I let the letter drop to the floor. Trash for the trash she is. Words echo in my head. From the street, or in the room itself. Breath shorter in my chest. But the sounds are from the backroom only. A mumbling. I push open the door. Herschel who never sleeps sits at his desk writing. The "holy" one. Mocking me with his pages filled with squares and circles. In-law, father-in-law, bound to me by rules and power. Making words into numbers. Letters mixed with letters, picked out from the holy books. Secrets from God's tongue only for him. Herschel whose lap as an infant Lea crawled into as if it were a better home than mine. Ignoring the urine and the crumbs.

His tongue clicks in his mouth as I stand over him. His pants are off again; his cuffs that I must wash stained with ink. The ageless legs veined blue but still strong. "Herschel, you must sleep," I whisper, but his hands move on unchanged. All this for nonsense, and his mouth always hungry to be fed. Herschel who people called the wise but who when I was a child in Volapzhin was only a strange one to be avoided. "He is thinking deep thoughts. Thoughts of God. Not for us," Papa said.

But why I thought should God not speak in our language but in words that made no sense? For all day through the town Herschel in his long black coat looked up at the sky or a nothing spot above the chimneytops. Chalking on walls messages I did not understand. *Tzaddik*, he wrote. *Sephirot, sefer, sippur*. And with fingers straight out his eyes went back till they were white as his chalk and his puppethands trembling. And even then I thought of his son: Jacob. What would he do with his father a shame and his mother having to sew to earn enough? For the pitying rabbi handed Herschel only a few pittance of coins as a gift.

Jacob too with his prophecies, mad plans for the future. Father like son, as they say. Newspapers he reads now—the *Tageblatt*, stories of Coney Island. Dreams uncoming of the Promised Land. Always a hoper, Jacob is, the sweet fool. A child with back bent, hair curling gray at the ends. But when you look to the heights, hold on to your hat.

"These gears that I make in the jewelry store," he said last week. "It is the same as the big rides there. *I* could build them too. New ones— The Crossover Track. The Firebird. A little money to start, that's all that I need. I will talk to the men at the synagogue."

I have heard all. "Why waste money on this? On your words no buildings can be built. We are getting old now. You have the watchstore. Enough. Sarah has moved to the Bronx. Judith to Flatbush. And yes our flat is better than most, no boarders no longer. But all our money you have 'invested' for your dreams, always gone and nothing back." The American way. Streets paved with money. Money taken from us. Go out at night it is tight to the ground no way of grabbing it.

"Why do you not want the things I want?" he asked.

I pursed my lips and was silent. Jacob like Herschel and the rabbis watching for signs in the sky and not this room with its roaches or the birch trees in Volapzhin where the road to Kiev curved. Remembering nothing of the work I do, the washing and scrubbing of the clothes. Heavy with water, hanging like Herschel's arms without shape, set to dry in the soot on the line. "With respect," Jacob says. But I have no respect for he who does not match his socks. Who does not know that someone else must match his socks.

Left to me the world as it is. The present and the past. The real knowing.

But there was a time when with Jacob gladly happily I went into the deep woods or behind the grainrows, his fingers soft on my back studying my skin as if to draw to sculpt. But here in the New World nights I said yes but only to endure. And so I swelled like a mushroom in the moss and eyes on my middle not my face. Already losing, passing. A weight to keep me from my flying. But for Jacob it was everything. Nights he would sit and kiss my swelled skin and tell stories to it. "Listen, child," he said. "You will be great. You will be beautiful. A house of your own. The world will be a dream that will come true. No monsters to fight. Growing straight and tall and strong."

Already his eyes turning in love towards this not yet a thing inside of me. Singing in a low voice no words just songs made of sounds as he had never sung to me. Then after the sweating and screams in the back room here at East Broadway the midwife Shaina held it up. And I thought, another thing has been taken from me, my body. They said, it is a girl. Lea. And only then I knew it was not a girl I wanted, a girl who would grow to look too much like me. Beautiful as I was beautiful, but not the same. Eyes like the ghost of my eyes, lips like the trace of my lips. Her life like a road, and the sun and her stepping quickly away.

She cried all night for what? Milk—me. Like the story Leib told, the Dybbuk that came in the darkness and drained the soul from you. I was a calf only to be milked. A curse on me after America, another curse. A burden still, she who will return tonight to ask me again to take her back. As if I had not already let her go from the first. As if she had not demanded it.

But sometimes there was more. To her I would sing in my voice that was not one of beauty. A daughter of Zion rocking her to sleep. Cooing of snow white goats and raisins and almonds. The sweet life of the past. And once she wanted the circus and I remembered the circuses that came to Volapzhin in the fall. I kissed her on the head and said, "Yes, we will go, together." On that day I changed into my red dress barely fitting anymore and taking her hand we walked through the streets and everything was beautiful. Lea pretty in her blue skirt and her face up to mine, mouth open as if to drink me in. Her hands copying, her eyes recording. When sometimes I do not want to remember or be remembered.

At the circus early we looked up at the red white and blue of the big top towering and smelled the gamy smell of the animals. In Lea's open eyes the same joy mirrored upwards as mine. By the animal pens we waited to pet the horses that pressed long snouts to our faces. Air hot through their nostrils, hair tough on their backs soft at the mane. Lea scared at first but when I patted them and they licked my hands expecting something not there, "Mama, mama pick me up," and I did. Wriggling in my hands she looked at the horse; the horse looked at her. Sad eyes demanding in the body of power. Mouth moving sideways to chew. Her hand out touching and laughing high she was light, light in my arms. I showed the elephants to her, trumpet trunks and white tusks flashing. "They are older than Grandpa Herschel," I said. Behind my dress she hid looking out. "See, they are like maps." Wrinkled with hills. Their eyes seeing back through the years. I had brought peanuts for Lea to toss to them, their trunkends rooting through the shells with gentleness, like the hands of a blindman on a face.

In our seats we waited for the organ to wheeze and blaze, our shoes sticking to the floor. For cotton candy Lea asked "Mama can I have some?" as the man moved past holding the pink clouds like sunsets on sticks. I called but already he was far too far but he will come again I said. You will get your candy. And the music started and first the clowns all in their many colors. Bright unlike the gray suits of everyone. Lea laughing at them acting so serious everything so much mattering but then always tripping falling water squirting. And in one tumble his red nose came off and stooping he picked it up and Lea's hand reached for my dress. Her eyes alive watching without fear.

Then the ringmaster in his black coat, applause and taking off his hat. Red vest smooth and soft but the brown middle button barely held by the threads. Easy he stood knowing he was master, whip in his hand. Why should there be him, why not clowns and then animals but instead he

pausing insisting we look at him in his cloak and his voice soft as if rubbing it across my arms? Not like the little circuses in Volapzhin, a family and a pony and a bear. The ringmaster father with gray hair, a rumpled jacket with dust on the shoulders. The child underfed older then me but no breasts yet balancing barely on a red ball, feet moving tip tip careful.

The horses galloped into the ring. "Look— look at the horses," I said to Lea. "There is the one you touched. There—your friend."

"Yes, yes," she said, but cannot speak more. Trotting around they came, full big horses and the rider in a dress long and trailing, beautiful as wave edges, white foam from the ship's back. But then it was happening again—a flash of black and crackle of wood on the edge of burning in Volapzhin. The horses swinging round, and the world gone dark in my eyes. Papa and the sliver of a swordblade descending. Blood on his chest. I was lost not seeing not hearing when the man passed again and Lea called "There, can I have my candy now?" Too late. Her eyes up on me pulling my hand hard till it hurt, like the anchor from the ship holding me down.

And now Lea not laughing but looking at me minute by minute. The animals the same as in Volapzhin but here suffering in sorrow. The horses beaten in the back, the dogs who do not jump through hoops as they should kicked and left to die. The dead following the circus train from town to town. And again I was fooled almost to joy. With the colors the noises of the crowd the animal blur pressing on me in pleasure but soon it is too much. It wants me to forget.

So when it was over with a sick feeling I did not try for Lea's cottoncandy. On the way out almost crying "What about the candy, mama?"

"It is too late," I said, not angry not wanting to hurt. "Next time."

There it is again. The voice. Not from my dreams but here, real. A cry not for help but beyond help. Half sob but more than sob. Sounding like a voice I have heard before. Rising from the street outside. I rush to the window. The buildings are dark, the streetlights off for the night. Nothing; no one.

Still I hear it, fainter now. I wrap the shawl

around my thickening shoulders, set my feet into my shoes, and unlatch the door. The hall is quiet, only the shuffle of Amira's heavy feet next door. The floorboards creak like a man moaning in pain. Step by step I go down through the darkness, feeling with my hands the fetid walls. Waiting for the rustle of the rats, bristle of their fur against ankleskin.

But they too must be asleep. Light leaks through the glass of the streetdoor. Slowly I turn the lock. Through the walls Mrs. Teplitsky's snores. Good.

Moonlight filters down the stone steps. Silence. The voice gone. Along East Broadway the building fronts repeat. Brick and stone and brick and stone. Thousands like me, asleep, and only I to hear this call.

Even now the streets are not empty. A man trudges through the darkness: a baker, a grocer. Never is there a time when work is not to be done. Even in the darkest crevice of the night. No Sabbath in this world. No rest from the moneymaking.

There: movement. In the darkness of the doorway across the way. Shadows: one or two, writhing, struggling. A sound as of a cough. I step off the stairs and am halfway across the street. Will I beat them about the head? Let loose a cry for the police?

But I reach the curb of the opposite side and in the doorway there is no one. Not even a young couple hiding for a kiss. Empty.

Everywhere there is suffering that no one notices. That no one hears. Calls in the night unanswered. The walkers on the streets deaf to the sobs. Who pass and see nothing.

And this the world that Lea wants to join! Sewing flags and fucking with the goy. When she comes tonight she will trail that filth into this room, talking of the future that is nothing but a lie. "Freedom," they say. Nothingword. Free. Free for these few blocks from Henry to Houston, in the Bronx from Mt. Eden to 176th. Our place to settle only. Pale. And the goy have everything. Money horses guns. And our rabbis cowards sighing saying nothing. Proclaiming that you must wait for the Promised Land that is a death. Speaking in Yiddish of the blessings of America: "We have come out of the land of bondeds" meaning bondage.

I wait one more minute for the cry to come again. But only silence. In shame I climb the stairs, a shade lighter now. Inside the room, the note from Lea still halffolded on the floor, a slight tremble in the cradlewood. A coo that is not of pleasant dreams but the outriders warning of tears oncoming. I look down at Avrom, left arm's fat folds thrown across his face. His chin is trembling, his mouth half opened, eyes wrinkling beneath angry furrows of brow. I take him up in my arms, sit in my chair and look at my face that peers from the mirror—a bargain of Jacob's, flecking and blistering with brown spots like the skin of the old woman I am not quite yet. Through the shadows I trace my wrinkles. Like mama in Volapzhin adjusting her scarf, roses and green stems. Mornings at the mirror, she wound it as I watched. Tucked by her chin, red like a scar. "Minna," she said, "You see it is beautiful. Colonel Kovalenko purchased it for me. A man in Kiev. A man who loved me. It is important to wear beautiful things. When I pass even the cows should think, there is a woman."

Mama was tall. Straight she sat in her chair. Her lip a line straight across her face. Her hair in grainwisps along the white fields of her cheeks. And then she bent and a sound came from her mouth, a cough of a Dybbuk deep inside. My hair wet and her eyes like stars falling coming apart but only tears. "Minna," she said, "There is no other world."

I crawled into her lap. A boat, I thought, the folds of her dress. I had not seen a boat, only pictures in a book that papa kept. We sailed together, mama and I. A river of roses. The scarf steeped with her tears. The boat of her dress rocking as her breath stormed, like when I stepped aboard the ship to America, from Hamburg after the harrowing from Kiev west. Wood it was, only wood, to hold back the sea, and this to be my home for the days till land. Dead and yet still moving as if alive when the storms roared. But after the week of blue blank, green humps on the world's edge. Rayna on the deck pressed her mouth to her boy's cheek, throwing her left arm up free as she cheered. I too caught in the hopewebs. First only wedges of color, hazed, then trees and grass, and then we were between two green cliffs and the bay before us. White sails. Birds glimmering on the waterskin. And shouts around me, secret voices from lips long silent. With others pressed, body, mind, voice. I took Jacob's hand. Quiet, eyes not yet believing. His face wet from spray. No, tears. Across the glare Manhattan, he said, woodspires of ships and docks.

But in the gleam suddenly the statue. Red firetip above the bronze going green. Jacob removing his hat, smiling through his beard. Miles and weeks on the water, here to be free, and no welcome but this they give, a statue? A giant too big to crush us, guarding the harborside. A queen, Tsarina with her crown, and America, Jacob said, a land with no Tsars. Already they bow, these fools gathered around me on the boatdeck. Always they are forgetting. Beat me, beat me! they cry. Ready to be serfs and servants again. Slaves to this new land as slaves to the old. "Give me your tired, your poor, your huddled masses yearning to breath free," I know now. Give me. And what is to be given to us in return?

So I should not have been surprised. Only one month after the voyageend, when the streets of this world were new, when we had nothing but our hunger, Rabbi Pelsner called me to his basement room at Eldridge and Canal. The doorway so low I had to duck to get inside. The rabbi nodding his head and squinting up his eyes as if this would convince me that he was a man of wisdom. Across the rightmost corner of his desk an overflow of dried white wax like a river frozen in its plunge in the wintertime. "You see," he said, "it is hard for the Jews in this new country. So many there are that do not want us. We must be careful so that they see the best of us. So you, a married woman with a husband, should not be walking the streets in these clothes that are not for outside wearing. Even if you are not a one to shave off your hair as the Lord says, at least to cover it. To wear dresses that reach below your ankles." His eyes that were heavy dropped to the bottoms of my legs.

So from the rabbi's room I went into the street and around me no one that I knew but only strangers and the world unlooking. What a greeting for this land! Wanting us all the same—gray in our sack cloths and my face fading with age like night coming on. Left inside like a shell forgotten. And then it was that I cried though I will not cry again.

I said, I will see this world. Despite all. Despite the rabbis and the henwomen, cowslow and grazing in gossip one to another. Sticking close when there was a world to be mapped. Each street to wander, block after block. To know this city that was forced on me.

So I walked, walked and looked. At the peddlers the same as in Volapzhin pushing westward along Grand, knifesscrapers crying harsh with voices ground like their knives. I followed them, hearing the pleas from the pushcarts selling rags and dirty fruit. Crates of eggs or candles for the home. Children tottering past, tossing pebbles and ground glass, whistling of cops. In the alleys playing with an old box and barrel, their mothers where? As we in Volapzhin, but the dirt there had been clean.

Everywhere as I walked the people were crowded close: cardplaying on stoops, laying the washing from high windows. Five floor buildings tightpacked, elbowing for room, metal cages running in Zs down the fronts. In storefronts on Clinton St. the barely more than *minyan* synagogues, chairs and a torah in the empty space. Ceilings of pressed tin in patterns. *Landsmanschafts*, so that each block each building was a spot on the map of the old world. Twenty minutes across Europe. Above Houston from B to the River, the Hungarians. Galicians between Houston and Broome, east of Clinton. Romanians west to Allen. And then for us from Grand Street south.

Into the windows of the stores past Essex I looked at the things that there were in America. The market shops like Solomon Gold's or Haracz and Sons with flat on their gravebeds of ice the schools of smoked fish—dull gray-brown herring and jewel bright salmon. More here than I had eaten in my entire life in Volapzhin. The floor soft with sawdust. The clerks bustling in crisp aprons. Outside the fatman barrels—sour and half-sour. Bursting in garlic juice with the teethbite. Tart on my tongue and turning my lips to white. Fritz the storeman reaching down to scoop the thickest

out for me in my red dress. When I was my most beautiful then.

Past the buildings with their windows shut where the women my age but no husbands would go to sew in the stifling heat. Returning late in the darkness with squinting eyes from threading needles and shoulders hunched further down each day. Molegirls who could choose only to live unmarried and then die.

I walked that day across Chrystie Street and down Bowery to Park Row to see for the first time the center of this world. The room at the maze heart, engines humming, shadowed even in the morning sun. The buildings so high that I could not breathe for fear of them falling. Up into the air when in Volapzhin the houses crept in rows along the ground. I thought, God will come to smite these men with their Babel towers. But when I looked up I could not help but laugh. For the buildings were not straight and serious like Rabbi Pelsner or Rabbi Meltzer, saying to the world you must see that I am a powerful man. Fifteen stories or more, but they played and joked like children. The red brick Tribune building striped with white stone like a package tied with ribbon. At the top off-center a spire pointing up. Taunting that it was so high. A boy waving proud from a treetop he had climbed.

I stood on the streetcorner, red in my dress. Hungry they watched me, the men from the stocks in their tight suits and hats all the same. Dead in their eyes in their pale faces. They looked. Jewess they knew perhaps but still beautiful. I looked at their looking. Feeling the heat in me, flushfull. Bird air lightness. I was more. Not Jacob's. Free. Back in the old woods, alone. Calico damp in summersweat on my legs, stockings soaked. For in their minds I could go with them past the signs saying "No Jews" or the nosigns meaning the same into their houses with thick carpets and carved darkwood. To see the uncut books on their shelves, the heavy couches with woodbacks curved like shipfronts.

But then he with the black hat came up to me, married I could tell. His wordbuzz of English I did not yet understand and I smiling with my lips but nothing more. His face was dark and secret, hand taking my hand even when he knew

I did not know his words. Close up he was old, pinchnosed, secret with sins and teeth like a field trampled by beasts. Hot breath stinking, rawwound mouth. And with his pocketpen I stabbed him or wanted to stab and watch his face bleed leaning in staggering paling and then all the men the same in their hats falling dead in America pen to their hearts. Blood in my hair on my dress red.

These were the men who ran the world. I watched, eyes open. Was this the Golden Land that Jacob brought me to? How is it better, different than Volapzhin? Only what has been lost. Stale air now and no trees. Noise and noise and the clocks ticking. Grayness falling on me in sleep. Or worse: the girls pressing to the windowedge; blueorange spark of flames bursting from behind. As it was in Volapzhin with the horsemen and papa. Death scattered everywhere like salt from a shaker.

I ran like a streak of light from City Hall back up East Broadway to collapse on a bench in Seward Park. So this was the world. This was to be my life. I watched the chessmen playing their games. Stooping suspendered to move sideways their black white knights. With Lea I listened to the speakers thundering of injustice to the scruffy crowds ignoring them. Beneath the brick stiff spine of the Library, towering in newness.

But how my memories muddle! The present presses. The years that came after nosing their way into the times before. No Lea of course in the first days of my walks. But no Seward Park either for there to be a library. Blocks of buildings not yet torn down, and the books in the basement rooms of the old Aguilar Library still smelling of mold and dust. No speakers in the Park, or if there was a Clara Lemlich then I did not know I did not know her.

Why do I have to think always of Lea? Of our days together, and what pleasures there might have been? I want to return to the years before unstained. To the New York when first I saw it. When I wandered the streets fresh without name, the voices without sense. Each strip of paper peeled back to the past, one atop another. Shops that have changed and fled, houses rising and falling. To get beneath the dirt of life and years built up. But I cannot forget what has come since. The nowness seeps back like roots going downward from air to earth, and brings no flowers. Smudging out the maps of what was.

But even then, at the first moment, when we stepped from Castle Garden, before the rabbi and Lea, it was too late. Always it is too late. For it is not this New World that I dream of. When in dreams I walk the lightstrip going forth, in terror it comes round circling. Taking me back only to where I was, tracing the wandering paths through Volapzhin, the shadows of the forest falling close. Even when I do not want to think of Volapzhin. Here the brick house of the Dubinsky's and there the post where they tied their dog where the rabbi used to stop on his walk home to talk over the Talmud with Berl the father. There the house where Basia lived where in the yard we would play Cossacks and throw each other down in the dirt and mud. And there the tree where Jacob and I met for the first time with heads up to look at the branches, golden curls and the turn of his gaze smiling. But then at the bend where the river nuzzles close to the road rightward a gray wall of fog of forgetting. Inside somewhere the slaughterhouse I know is there but the size and color gone. Wood or stone? Pigs or cows or what? No more the stifled grunts, terror of eyes I must have heard or seen. All faded as in the spring the mist would rise off the river and only the housetops clear. Blotted, blurred, and who knows what beyond.

I stand at the edge of the water and look back at what is drowned and drowning. I want to see again, to remember. Not just Lea, her remnants and reminders. But Volapzhin: as in my New World walks at every streetbend the town comes to me in pieces. Sunset reflections from the synagogue in the glint in the glass of a storefront. The waste of cloth in the streetgutter, bright as in the top drawer of mama's dresser. From scraps I could sew, if I could sew in light, and the Old World would return. Stitch after stitch into coat or cloak. Market streets on the arms and the smell of horses at the hems. In fabric shimmering of many colors and patterns and shapes. Around my shoulders I place it, soft on my skin, and again I am at home in anywhere, walking the streets as they were. But like water it slips from my back,

sinking into the earth, and my eyes open only to New York and the dawn.

APHORISMS
by Kevin Griffith

_____

You cannot use light to see the light.

Even a bottomless pit has a top.

Absurdity: The sound of one god clapping.

There can never be a partial whole.

How long ago was before time began?

Do I look fat in this paradox?

No matter how many birds you use, you cannot kill even one stone.

The life you want is always longer than the one you have.

Eternity stays open during the pandemic.

There's no place like nowhere.

The river's answer to everything is more river.

I can't say enough about silence.

ANSWERS TO NON-EXISTENT QUESTIONS
by Kevin Griffith

———————————

Because the snow can never cover itself.

Because the doll in the coffin opens its eyes.

*

Because hope survives by using the body of a moth as its raft.

*

Because a beached cloud dies on your lawn.

Because when water drowns, you will never find the body.

Because the balloon holds an old man's last breath.

*

Because dust becomes us when it dies.

*

Because this morning is drawn by a child with no hands.

Because a fly is a saint washing his hands with sunlight.

*

Because every day the dark dies in its sleep.

CREPUSCULAR

by Kevin Griffith

Darkness approaches the lip
Of the waterfall.

Tiny claws grasp for purchase,
Hold the gray leaves of sage
That smile through their own fur.

And a prayer blows down
the street—a whisper that has swallowed
its own echo.

WOLF TICKETS THROUGH THE FERAL WINTER
(excerpt from *Feverglades*)
by Kirk Marshall

The dogs were muscling their gaunt shapely forms from out of blind snow-bracketed banks, lanes, ditches, Detroit's steel-girdered intersticies—the inglenooks and modesties of Dearborn, slender brown skulk like clats of sinister inchworms on the eye. Their bellies cinched in dry lank starvation. Their ears and snouts and coats kinked wet, glossed, obtaining an august diesel sheen in the glaucous boreal light, blue kidney figments as though migrant dolphins come ashore on roaming silver-haired legs. A thousand thousand hounds surface loping along the grey march. Their tongues pink and exposed and ice-chafed, whiskered muzzles zebraic with facets of cloven white. Their gums scalloped a darker pink, their gums bared and gnarled a traumatic hue, their gums clustered with milky crescent teeth. Pelted and knickerbockered a variation of colour, a mottle of browns, reds, rusts, yellows, silvers, blues. Coats to pillow the eye. Lemons and whiskeys and jets and gold oxides all assembling in unpeopled streets striated fire-pure and barren with snow coral. Old winter-feasted trees, choke cherries and aspens ailing and sharded in the godless thaw, holly and gold hyssop and shimmering sneezeweed felled low before the raptured greening, now trembling to herald the arrival of the dogs.

Snowflakes wheeled loose from snickering branches. Skinny Dinners stood watch, binoculars slack in the curvature of his neck, his hands balled under his singlet, his heart aching with a sweet local thunder.

He was stationed on the arch above Michigan Avenue, the strange primal terrain divested before him, and he could see all the way westward over half-collapsed factory rooftops, past shuttered bodyshop compounds and looted junkyard plots, beyond needle-littered stripmalls and uninviting newspapered Miller bars, all the way to the green pasteurised waters of the lower soak of the River Rouge. Skinny's nose was streaming, his knuckles aching with cold, his ears numbed an urgent shade of red. His teeth, misaligned and granular, were tweezering through the green husks of nuts, pistachio cloves and pepitas. He chewed his sockets of shivered savouries, greeted the all-invasive freeze, and calculated. He was counting the dogs as they advanced.

He knew he could only take a small sample of their starving contingent, which is to say: father a few. He'd steeled himself for the inevitable heartbreak, compelled himself to reconcile with the articles of necessity and accept that he would have to abandon more than he could shelter and strengthen, but now seeing the dogs in their proliferating numbers, the Messiah of Curs shrank to assume ownership for the sweet displacement of a newly-toasted pain in his chest, felt the heft of damage invoked by renewing the hope of the dogs, only to suffer the tungsten char of repeated rejection. Most would get one meal free, and no more. He couldn't provide for them all, and they couldn't all accompany Skinny on his mission for revenge. It was a congenital weakness in him, some freely-rooted defect in the soul that he would always fall in love with every dog he ever met. He couldn't muster the same interminable warmth for people, whom he felt were perversions of electricity and sinew, aberrated mammals of alien inelegance, weird inheritors whom cannibalised the land and walked upright on hind legs as if it substituted for civility. Mankind made Skinny fulminate; he would allow himself and everyone he'd finagled to befriend against his better knowledge to be eaten alive, if it were the dogs supping their fill on his vitiligoid flesh, their tongues laving his blood, their teeth cracking open his sour stalky bones.

He would defer to the governance of the dogs at any second, untroubled by questions of ontology or human solidarity, if only one vengeful cur vaulted a neighbourhood fence to recruit Skinny for an assault on his own society: If the mutts intimated that they were prepared to re-cover what the people had lay claim to long ago, the earth and its fecund loping grounds, Skinny would coerce his own mother to surrender her-self to the toothy meat-bated mouths.

And yet he knew to disclose as much to a lover or a professional quack earmarked him as crazy. He didn't mind. The diagnosis of psycho-logical pathologies, maladies and human neuro-ses wasn't a valuable discourse for Skinny, because doctors were always prescribing the treatment of symptoms and never the rudimentary cause: people had deprived dogs their inheritance, and eventually people fell ill from terminal guilt. It was a silent genocide, an invisible enslavement, an enforced suppression as storied as time imme-morial. Willing loyalty from the dogs had become insidious tradition, was a crime too habituated to rectify. What were the dogs to do? They were companionable animals with uncomplicated agendas; they conformed to a legacy of subor-dination because it was in their nature to please. They fawned when defiance was needed. They pawed where they should protest. They content-ed themselves with lives of sedated domesticity, gnawed their scrotums on cool linoleum and grovelled for the favour of their masters.

Skinny saw all this and despised people all the more for it, felt complicit in the systemic sub-jugation of a guileless species, superior creatures of susceptible natures. Such a conclusion was not merely arrived at because of a truant youth mis-spent reading paperback Marxist theory, or from years seething beneath exploitation documen-taries of dogfighting and indiscriminate canine culls. Skinny Dinners had witnessed it firsthand throughout his twenties, many times over: he'd observed dogs being variously euthanised or tormented, abused or abandoned in his travels through Vietnam, Thailand, Laos, South Korea, India, China, East Africa, Egypt, Russia, Roma-nia, Brazil, Mexico, even fucking Canada—the fiery injustice had assumed a fever pitch intensi-ty in him in an inner-city street in Johannesburg when he'd seen a dog shot dead in a doorway, and he'd almost convinced himself that he must be haunting a film devised by Tarkovsky or Bela Tarr, because the combustive echoes of that gun-shot ricocheted in his mind for weeks. It was a wholesale sadism, enough to compel Nietzsche to succumb to agonising madness. Yet Skinny had become resolved in a conviction that he would help restore the balance, somehow, when the soonest occasion demanded it.

Surveying this ocean of sleek torpedo bod-ies from above the snow-frescoed archway over Michigan Avenue, confronted by the yowling throng of malnourished mongrels and bitches and sewer-sequestered strays swarming to receive instruction, Skinny was sure he could endow a few with the deliverance they deserved. It tor-tured him to enlist the services of those he sought to emancipate, but it was the easiest way that he could contrive to set them upon their enemy. He would engineer the right circumstances for the dogs to deliver the opening *mêlée*, the immediate gambit, to steward them to win their own back against humanity. He would feed his enemies to the dogs—this way he might hope to grow that much closer to becoming one with the pureheart-ed quadrupedal breed, earn himself some insin-uated status amongst the louse-riddled under-class, the underdogs surfacing to chokehold their benevolent dictators finally, finally, finally. He would watch people he knew be encircled by co-lourblind carnivores half-retarded by mange and ringworm, and he would not seek to intervene while he heeded the sight of blood-slick human fingers twitching between the jaws of the dogs.

This dream of emaciated canines feasting, their tails scissoring in frenzied pack sentience, elicited a smile on Skinny's raw skewbald features.

He was mentally inventorying the dogs as they padded toward the overpass, his cheeks puckered with nut husks, taxonomising those whose size, physicality, speed, gait or character appealed to him especially: he loved them all with an instantaneous and almost erotomaniac inten-sity, of course, and he was loath to apply a Dar-winian criterion to matters of the heart, but he found he could simultaneously quantify his rap-ture by fractions and degrees while harbouring affection for them all with equal vehemence. So that Skinny could project an intellectual graphic

in his mind's eye upon which each dog clustering beneath the overpass was ascribed a subjective numerical value, as befitted a personal formulae of his own devising: each quotient would be used to grade the primacy of the dogs, their essential perfection. He found that this was the most psychologically economical method to determine which of the wild conscripts in this colony of curs demanded immediate recruitment. Those most distinguished animals he could rely on to retaliate against the quarry they might hunt in a wholly decisive manner.

Such monsters would exercise their own pedigree of feral reckoning. For Skinny, it would be like releasing a virulent taint of rabies into the soft, blushing, overestimated heart of America. The mind of his motherland would seize, would paralyse from poison transfer, this terrific pox on leathered feet sent to zombify the pockets of patriots who cowered in hiding. The dogs would make amends. He would endue on them new unspoiled horizons overburdened with bones.

There were twelve hounds that were elevated by the functions of his formulae. Skinny shifted his weight on the rampart above the slender wraiths with their exposed ribcages and panting snouts, began pacing the parapet with erratic purpose. The dogs began to whine, to bay at his hovering silhouette. His pillowy white high-tops parsed through the snow soup like the footfalls of a wolf-god, a forest-blazered demagogue of winter legend. He began allocating the twelve with names, his blood coursing, his breath ragged, the wind whipping its whitenesses through his rust-squirrelled skull fuzz. He spoke the names now, at a whisper and into his jacket collar, just to hear the music they made sweep through the keyholes and flues and conveyor belt turbines and wine glasses of every shuttered business in decaying, desolated Dearborn. They charmed the mouth to invoke their sounds. They tickled Skinny's synapses as if vanilla vodka in the gut.

Ganymede. Mimas. Calypso. Callisto. Leda. Titan. Juliet. Nix. Galatea. Neso. Skoll. Arche.

Names used to incite a war, names used to claim the most starrily-fortified night skies. He grinned, an event so rare and nightmarish that the dogs amassed in the streets were momentarily silenced. Skinny Dinners clapped his palms together, drummed his chest, whistled on his fingertips. He extended his hands high above his head, an effigy of Nixon pandering on the accordion stairs of Air Force One, and howled.

The dogs responded with the fullness of their tautened throats, harmonising to entertain one fell canine lament which stirred flakes from the knots of the trees.

Then Skinny bent low, feathered open the folds of his rucksack, and retrieved a plastic assemblage of 3D-printed photopolymer parts, an inoffensive jigsaw of violin-contoured acrylic, and swiftly wrested together the weapon he'd smuggled through airport security. The gun was a bone white mould, an amalgam of resinous pivots and dovetails. It was mounted on his shoulder in no more than two minutes.

Skinny scoured the ground and the rippled overpass paving beneath his feet with momentary irritation: a splay of yards from where he was stationed, his eye caught the refractive glint of syringe glass, and he exhaled, nodding.

Skinny dismounted the overpass platform, and crunched up with deliberate satisfaction toward the hypodermic needle discarded in the wet grey sludge heaped by the archway. Its flute was intact, unsullied by hairline cracks, the glass filament unbroken. He folded to a monastic crouch, his fingers moving with surgical caution, before extracting the syringe from the junk-laden culvert. Again, he nodded his head with indiscernible gratitude, while nesting the needle in the woollen hasp of his hand. He plundered his inner jacket pocket with his free hand, and came out flourishing a screwtop bottle of liquid acepromazine formula, its innocuous over-the-counter label cautioning Skinny to safeguard the drugstore sedative from the reach of children. Oh for the unsuspecting little darlings he would sneakily administer doses to if time and evil were on his side!

Skinny uncapped the bottle of ACP, evacuated the milky residue trapped in the cannula with a pivot of the plunger, and inserted the needle's bevelled flute into the clear iodised liquid. He drew up an ampule of the fluid formula into the glass barrel, jetted the runoff in a flick of the needle valve, and palmed the syringe into the magazine of his piecemeal phosphor-tinted gun with a clean roll of the wrist.

The syringe clicked snugly into the chamber of Skinny's jigsaw firearm with impossible cooperation, a curious synergy engineered by design. His squared jaw softened, and something like a dance of warm sufficiency seized his witchy black pupils.

If a vagrant spectator in downtown Dearborn were to observe this tiger-banded albino apparition with his scalp of red furze and the burn scarring, he or she might have concluded it an odd tableau when the gaunt figure tracked back down the snow-lustred arch, before mounting a matte-white air rifle on the overpass, and directing its deathly snout at the dogs clamouring for amity beneath him.

Such a witness would recognise that what next eventuated was the waging of some ominous gambit, but he or she would be remiss not to concede that there was an apocalyptic poetry to the light cold scene, as if a final glory rendered by Brueghel before consumption. Snow was lashing the bloodless tousled magnolias shading the intersection, ice veins depraving the convalescing old trees, and two or three wildfowl careening green and scarlet visited the hushed polar sidewalks, a fletch of pheasants who flushed east toward the riverfront. They susurrated and were gone, a rainbow optic in the endless rushing white.

Skinny Dinners did not engage in melancholic reflection, but merely breathed ghosts above the avenue as he augured himself on his haunches. He squirmed momentarily beneath the weight distribution of the gun, adjusting its pennyweight frame, and sighted along the crosshair until it lined up with his quarry. The nut cloves in his mouth were now paste. His nose was wet with mucal ooze, and the hint of a sinus headache spiralled warningly behind his right eye. He blinked thrice in rapid succession, and slackened his triggerhold.

A sudden sadness sprang unbidden in the lean meat of his chest, a mournful resign that swallowed his heart. Skinny Dinners inured himself to a legacy of travesties, bunked down in the raw sorrow that his friends and employers had betrayed his loyalty, incited him into wolfish action, forced his fire-bitten hand. He could see that acid wash alone would lubricate his future, that from here the particulars of his behaviour would be ugly and inhumane.

His knuckles grew empurpled. His earlobes burned a hundred injustices.

Skinny Dinners finally relented to his quashed dog nature: he was yearning to break off the leash, root out every rat. His brow thundered. He pulled the trigger. A shot rang out, a whip-crack of fricative sound sundering the still of the smoking white horizon.

For an eternity no movement followed, the rupture shocking the shrunken world into unvoiced allegation. Echoes surfed the hackles of every dog, terrified and snarling, their bellies peeling across the frozen asphalt. Skinny waited and the whiteness fell, and Skinny waited and the dogs scrambled, and Skinny waited and the snowflakes suffocated the bark of supple green pines like clover, and Skinny waited and the River Rouge curled into the black forge of denuded, decay-eaten Detroit. Skinny remained chest-in-the-snow, and the gun eased back into his armlock, skating against the inside of his forearm, and kinesis was restored to the world, the gunshot disbursed to ever fainter whispers, and a million street dogs retreated snapping, yelping, keening, snarling, into the covert quadrants of the city.

He felt shamed as they wheeled about scattering; he was soul-deep in moral quicksand, invaded by a rank blue funk of self-disgust. He palmed an errant snowflake from his eye.

The dog he'd shot, the freshly-improvised syringe dart sutured in its rising black flank, was slumped in the chum-flooded junction of the emptying avenue, its whimpers reduced to a plosive falsetto coo. Skinny drew his binoculars to his catty gaze, and squinted for definition, for confirmation, through the lens. The dog in question was a soft sable mass on the crosswalk, depleted—at least in this instant—of war and gamble and warm animal terror, no red clapping maw, no ears flattened and back legs scoring furrows in the frost. The intravenous sedative had worked its magic into the black beast's churning sinewy interior. Skinny understood enough about the science

to know that he had whole minutes to act, and if he waited any longer an armoured fleet of cops in blue fatigues was certain to materialise along the sidewalk besides.

He was limited to this opportunity, this sole ploy, this merest distance of yards, now.

He didn't linger over dismantling the photo-polymer air rifle, but merely dispatched the readily assembled firearm into his rucksack, along with the few rubber-stoppered buckets of chum stock remaining, and pocketed the phial of ACP in the armpit of his jacket. He was brisking along the embankment, and then he was navigating the stairs two at a time as they corkscrewed their way back toward the steaming reaches of Michigan Avenue. The satchel rattled against his shoulder, administering an unpleasant coldness to the pale flesh of his neck, but he was springing now, fanging his way toward the bottom while his sneakers of flossy Hoth husbandry avoided assuming impact with the cement for more than the briefest glances. Skinny was virtually lemur-born, such was the impression elicited by his long-limbed agility, because he was so svelte in his movements now that the snow seemed not to catch him, a lithe white star of track and field, a baby-faced harlequin of spidery graces.

He had made it to the foot of the colonnade again, was hustling at street level toward the horsey beast asleep at the snow-bottled intersection, the dog in its soporific muddle of pelt fleece and black fat, a plaintive homily quaking in its throat.

Skinny slowed down to a stroll, his heart craving collapse and his lungs swimming in his chest, and he coasted forward through the debris of gore until he was sidling pussyfooted around his beautiful barrel-sized trophy, its kingly head at rest on its forelegs, eyes half-slack with enigmatic quiet.

The dog was a grizzled male Plott hound, a colt-like giant enthroned in a soapy black coat, an imperious saunter about the eyes, two intelligent garnet facets. He had seas to swim, bears to hunt, moats to besiege. He was Skinny's great new beloved, a fairytale inamorato the size of a monster Buick. The dog boomed a little more darkly, a little more saxophonic at Skinny's elegant approach, but it did not wrestle to right itself, merely snorted its shining globular muzzle as the unfamiliar threat announced himself with continued stealth.

The dog watched, its majestic corduroy ears tented in surprise, as the Messiah of Curs retreated a distance of ten feet away before bustling to sit down, squat and attentive, the man's wine-dappled face an artefact of trusting observation.

The dog and Skinny Dinners sat at a reversed convex angle whole body lengths apart for at least seven minutes. Skinny's breath softened, assumed distinctly sinuous shapes. The Plott hound cocked its head quizzically, yowled in discomfort, and pawed at the snow where it sprawled. Gradually the dog inched forward in playful prostration, surfing its glossy onyx musculature through the snow, until it was a hand's breadth away from Skinny and whining mournfully for his ministrations.

The dog's hot noxious breath blew against his pillowy cold clavicle, and moulded over his bristled dome. Skinny continued maintaining a quarter-mile stare in the opposite direction. The dog was now strafing its moist snout through his hair, exhaling the sweet spiced fetor of loss into the warm splint of his inner ear, but Skinny did not grin again or edify the courtship until the dog dangled its head into his lap, and surrendered to his better wisdom.

Skinny's fingers sunk into its pelt, jiggered the beast from under the chin. The dog was moaning now, willing his strange benefactor to retrieve the tranquilliser steeled in its hide.

Skinny Dinners cajoled soft promises to the dog, the man's face buried in its dark marzipan coat, his mouth disclosing a serenade into its nobly sloping ears. There was a smile in his voice, but the dog knew the words the man spoke signified a therapeutic truth.

'Who's a good boy? You're a swell good boy. When we get to where we're going, I'm gonna name you Ganymede,' Skinny lullabied, massaging the dog's ears.

'Now, Ganymede, what I have to do for you is going to sting like a hoary old hornet in the nutsack. But I can't leave this needle in your side, you understand? Any longer in you, and there's

danger of a seizure risk or an epileptic complication, you hear me? This thing's gotta go, and you and I gotta walk, okay?'

The dog understood the articles being negotiated. The man was calm, and kind, and resourceful, and an emissary for future meals—so much food to sweat the throat. The dog knew to subscribe to the man's rationale was to exercise the most advantageous tactic. Befriending the man would save its life, winch it away from the seething white barbarism of a final winter.

The dog knew what should happen. When the man's cool soothing hand closed around the haft of the needle, Ganymede thought only of the foliage on the trees enveloping Michigan Avenue as they rustled beneath the snowfall, watched the choke cherries and the aspens, bone white as ivory, submit themselves to the weight of their bitter cloak, and he couldn't sense there was any other way, no time in all of history for even one defector, one exception—just a rule as old as centuries. Ganymede transferred his own eyes to those rooted high in the kind man's head, and suddenly the cold, the ancient cold in the thrall of its element, was rushing in, every storm in every century, snaking its way through the interred roots of the magnolias to lance its way through the wound in his flank. The dog howled, its colossal black head thrust back in bright electric throttles of pain, and the earth kept its axial spin, not even slowing in its severe sickled mission to make its demands of everyone before they could even think to fall into line.

The trees bowed, the snow fell.

Some time later the man and his dog set to limping up the highway.

ELSEWHERE

by Nathaniel Calhoun

---

into a swarm provoked glowers a shade
through whom light tears.
towards the rut an outlier lowers, hoarse
in the dimpled pew for the damp coda of known loss.
a wayward strafer loiters by a crux deriving odds.
one dagger strike, quarterly, suffers the substitute muse—
elsewhered past reckoning.
a warrior wanders unreachable with frayed leads—
weight shedding as anchors, severed to sink in the seabed.

beneath notice the heart's elastic sags,
found wanting currency. spare tires trade
on a common market, storied with steel belts.

bereft the rift where a beckoning gathered
that wafted off in an infant breeze.
the ungrasped antidote lathers away
leaving cracks to dry. under layers of crashed wave
settles an erratic son, shorn of formal caring.

everything I fed to her fire burned up,
my furnace with it, however precious to me.
ash tithed lovingly to a coddled sapling
torn up when the house is sold.

through a crag where the barricade sinks
in the mud of yesterday's downpour slides
a creature unconcerned. out of mind and slighted
staggers an aspirant bond, sundered to the quick.

onto the pyre with a pulse, a widow prodded
from living memory—crowds climb toward limelight.
animals catch the whispered rue, process our leveling
with side eyes.

down the river and also ablaze
goes a boat that won't find her way homeward.
sometimes we find ourselves on a causeway of sorrows
and that is where our feet fall for a while.

BRACTS

by Nathaniel Calhoun

---

gaze enough upon the sea and whales breach.
a monstrance twinkles from the riverbed
of realtime numbers. watch your orchid closely
and you won't miss the instant of her blooming.

these moments could be simulated—
slowed, multiplied, magnified, saturated,
sold, resequenced, scored, altered, sharpened
and dulled. appetite curdles in recrimination
at the prospect of such surfeiting.
proliferations conjure a too-seedy wattle.

dandelion bracts plucked from the sky
dry to the windowpanes. crimson leaves
outlive their own memories, pressed
unfulfilled between the pages

what trace remains of yesterday's lowtide footprints?
is now a technical question:
whose property passed overhead
at what resolution contending with which
cloud conditions and how backed up
or accessible? satellites have reached
the moment of stars—plentiful enough
that their naming conforms to coded logic—
narrative retires, expecting little else,
after beating the archetypes to death.

an orca props her chin upon a rock to peer
patiently at a fisherman—then slides home
without splashing. airborne dolphins
at a distance mirror the calligraphy
of mayflies impressed upon the ceiling tiles,
lightly smudged—fixed above the white caps.

there are times when I turn away
from an unruly sea as one might dissociate
near a shopper losing his cool
in some public space.

STUCK

by Nathaniel Calhoun

───────────────

stuck lacks discipline and inventory
to resolve injury, tithes to favored
daydreams, gawks in the observatory.
stuck is a losing hand in someone else's
story of money—optionlessness dappled
with narrow promises of exceptionalism.

the replay mentality pestles, cudgels,
jackhammers—longing to access
earlier chapters anew. heavy steps
in soggy earth—riptides of an addled mind.

put what's in the fridge on the table,
put what's on the table in the face,
clean the area. tremble before avoidable consequence,
see rot where there isn't, enfold the siege layer,
compete for his sunlight and breath his air.

moments flood the indices. synonym after synonym
pile atop misspellings sourced from every assumption.
moments masked in idiom, cross-referenced
mercilessly, rut the guidelines, scour the damp ground,
bidding to become rivers, rising to become torrents,
longing to leap back into the sky.

in rapids anything stuck is worn away.
along the seaside anything stuck is worn away.
not so with tungsten trauma conducting nightmare's
burly grudge. harm feuds, welded sharp upon synapses,
modified to accept unforeseen power sources—
poached moments spackled to partitions
within a fractal coast of bog and briar.
peptides run hot towards a heat death of their own.

fragments validate a time of gathering.
which cycles govern the seeds of this unripe moment?
those times of paddling in place, were they bravery
or blindness?

every bonsai relationship is mutual.

BACK CHANNELS

by Nathaniel Calhoun

during a palladium fortnight the repositories
glide over smooth water guided by choice servants
who agree on back channels to avoid one another
in a world we see as mineral crumbs.

screaming issues from a voluntary portal
another cabin cancels all sound
in a third the grunt of shock royalty fucking—
law of the sea, selling point of boats.

the shimmering exaggerate strain,
rechristen normalcy with modern names
and borrowed body art—longing to be pharaohs—
plowing back into the earth their fallow men.

it seems we are best understood as a desiccant
straining for the moisture of others
that we might salt it and mark thereby
the area of our sad happening.

there is a cult of dampening that hovers
in the gulped moment of its own noise
sponsoring towers where avid minds pull
telepathy from apes with a fanfare
of marvelous wire—the precursor
to superimposition—strung from
the universe of having back
into the universe of want.

I have bought several roosters and
paid extra that they be handed to me
oven-ready, enjoying, after,
my neighbor's deference and the quiet.

MONEYED HYPOTHESIS

by Nathaniel Calhoun

———————————

beneath the moneyed hypothesis
of choice gallivanting
the whole corporate experiment trails off
having failed to produce worthy insight.

yachts slick the waters
holding something down at all times.
godlings poach consequentially
now wrapped tightly next billowing.

the soft spoken theory of change:
delight the wealthy serve their ambitions
and they may favor your plans
pending adequate supplication.
imagine their consoles
the fuel in their tanks
their whole dumpster flock of eyeballs.
some find their way to transformation
through such portals.

I don't know where to allocate significance:
the stretching or the tension
the healing or the heft of daring men.

I chase safety in the midst of leopards
a weapon without a turret
or a turret without a weapon.

MICROMORTS

by Veronica Tang

---

0 micromorts

Stubbed toes, LSD, papercuts, and cigarettes.

Mathematically defined as the one-in-a-million chance of death, micromorts were created to measure the "riskiness of various day-to-day activities."

And since no activity is without risk, zero micromorts should not exist. After all, what would a life without risk look like? Isolation in a padded room, trapped behind bulletproof glass in a museum? Simply put, disconnected. Disconnected from this reality, at the very least. Even getting out of the bed at twenty years old is one micromort. That is to say, one out of a million twenty-year-olds die getting out of bed.

But because micromorts are a mathematically defined unit, zero does, in fact, exist. The micromorts of any given activity is calculated by taking the number of deaths due to said activity, dividing by the population in question, and multiplying by one million. Therefore, if any one activity has never killed a single member of the population, say, stubbing a toe, the micromorts of that activity is 0.

By that argument then, the risks of taking LSD and dying from a papercut are equivalent. *Am I the only one who thinks that is stupid?* Even better, they are both equal to zero.

You see, this is the result of an unfortunate oversight. Smoking a single cigarette will not kill you immediately, but enough cigarettes will eventually do the trick. Some say to add one micromort for every 1.4 cigarettes you smoke—*how the hell does that even work*—while some particularly picky statisticians measure chronic risks with mi-

crolives, units of risk representing half an hour of change in life expectancy. But these are even more dubious, because they are calculated with rough estimates based on the assumption that, for small enough risks, the change in life expectancy is roughly linear.

Ronald A. Howard is a professor at Stanford and holds a Bachelor of Science degree from MIT. Fat lot of good it did him, because this is anything but a science.

The final flaw lies in the definition of risk—one assumes that all we have to risk is life, that our perception of risk is based on the possibility of death. But I'd like to argue that as humans, we have much, much more to lose than just our lives. *Or else the concept of sacrifice would be foreign to us.*

Victoria Leigh Soto is an American teacher who was murdered in the Sandy Hook Elementary School shooting while protecting her students. But to act in such a way that puts herself at risk? The only explanation in game theory is that she acted irrationally.

9 Micromorts

Skydiving in the U.S. is about 9 micromorts per dive.

Wendy wanted to go with Peter. To see the land he spoke of, to be a child forever in Neverland. But how could she, when she did not know how to fly?

"I'll teach you," he said, and he held her hands as he drew her to the window.

"Oh, how lovely to fly."

"I'll teach you how to jump on the wind's back, and then away we go."

J.M. Barrie described it as "heavenly", and I can't help but wonder what it feels like too. I imagine that flying or skydiving must feel a little bit like skating: weightless, exhilarating, the physical embodiment of a dream. I gave up my white leather skates nearly a decade ago, but even now, the jumps and spins that were once second nature to me remain in my body as residues of a past life, ingrained in my muscle memory. From time to time I dream of it still, the comfort of ice beneath my feet, wind in my face, and the world blurring past my watering eyes.

"So come with me, where dreams are born, and time is never planned. Just think of happy things, and your heart will fly on wings, forever, in Never Never Land."

They say it is the thrill that is addicting. *Thrill? What thrill? Only nine in a million die. How can there be a thrill? Where does the adrenaline come from in that place of utter safety?*

Realistically speaking, most of us will never encounter any activity with more than three digits of micromorts—in this day and age, we have learned to live without fearing for our lives, learned to live in complacency. Because what dangers can compare to the challenges our ancestors faced? We do not live in caves, run from predators, or scavenge for food. The circumstances that forced us to evolve into the species we are today no longer exist. Indeed, the tiny range of micromorts we live our lives within have ensured the unchanging nature of *Homo sapiens sapiens.*

But though the risk of dying for the modern human is remarkably small, death will come for each and every one of us eventually. *Will she come as the Morrigan, phantom queen of the Irish Ulster Cycle, covered head to toe in the feathers of a crow?* Until then, we entertain ourselves with illusions, foolishly believing that by hurtling through the air or by balancing on metal blades, we can challenge death itself.

Peter held the arrow that felled Wendy in his hand. "She is dead," he said uncomfortably. "Perhaps she is frightened at being dead." I'd like to think that, for a moment, Tinker Bell might have felt a twinge of regret. But J.M. Barrie knows best, and according to him, "fairies have to be one thing or the other, because being so small they unfortunately have room for only one feeling at a time."

Victory, then. Just victory, intertwined with death inside the fairy's mind.

22 Micromorts

22 micromorts per day. All causes of death. In general. In the United States, at least.

Here is a number that quantifies the risk of dying in any given day. Do we do this out of fear, to try to predict what we cannot control?

They say this is from "all causes." Then theoretically, this is a summation, no? People who died from shark attacks plus the people who died from drowning minus the people who died from both. *There, now it follows Inclusion-Exclusion Principle.* But where are the people who died from heartbreak? From loneliness? From unrequited love? *Oh, hang on, it's right here: the risk of suicide is 0.3 micromorts per day. For non-natural causes in general, 1.6 micromorts per day.*

Every time a child says, "I don't believe in fairies," there is a fairy somewhere that falls down dead. Clearly, Tinker Bell died from non-natural causes too. *How unlucky! Only 1.6 out of a million.*

48 Micromorts

48 micromorts per year. Murder and non-negligent manslaughter in the United States. Funny how this number is only 10 for the UK and 15 for Canada, huh?

By the same logic that we applied to Tinker Bell, according to FBI Table 16, Victoria Leigh Soto died from a gunshot. Not from *agape*, the unconditional love both Greeks and Christians dreamed of.

They say that when children die, Peter Pan goes part of the way with them so that they will not be afraid. I hope he taught them to fly, the twenty first grade children who died with Ms. Soto.

All children, except one, grow up. Well, I hope you shared your adventure with them too, Peter, because I don't think they'll grow up either.

"There never was a simpler, happier family until the coming of Peter Pan."

430 Micromorts

All causes, the first day of life.

The first day of life is also the deadliest. Why do statistics hate children so much?

Peter Pan once ran away to live among the

fairies in Kensington Gardens. "You see, Wendy, when the first baby laughed for the first time, its laugh broke into a thousand pieces, and they all went skipping about, and that was the beginning of fairies."

I was born a month early with a full head of hair, but apart from that, nothing was wrong. Still, I get the feeling that I hated stats as much as they hated me, because danger emerged for the first time when I was seven, which is theoretically the safest age to be in the United States. It was either lose the skin on my arm or risk skin cancer, and I chose the latter, because I wanted to be free to move and breathe and laugh and dance. Thankfully, that gamble has paid off.

Wendy told her mother that a new fairy is born each time a new baby laughs. Just as there will always be new babies, there will always be new fairies. But of the 430 out of a million children destined to die within 24 hours of birth, how many live long enough to laugh?

37,932 Micromorts

Mt. Everest. 37,932 micromorts per ascent attempt.

The mountain has claimed the lives of many. 37,932 deaths for every million people that attempt the climb. Well, I suppose this is the tax they must pay to reach the top of the world. Cold, snow, oxygen-deprivation, exhaustion.

So beware all adventure seekers, unless you see the world the same way Peter does: "To die will be an awfully big adventure."

500,000 Micromorts

What psychopathic maniac are we talking about here?

Only one thing comes to mind for a number this high, and it's marrying Henry VIII. That, or flipping an ideal coin and shooting someone for every tails.

> *Boleyn and Howard lost their heads,*
> *Anne of Cleves he would not bed,*

> *Jane Seymour gave him a son—but died before the week was done,*
> *Aragon he did divorce,*
> *Which just left Catherine Parr, of course!*

I was born the day Anne Boleyn should have died, on the 18th of May. I've always admired her daughter, the little red-headed girl who would grow up to rule nations and defeat armadas. But really, it's a pity, because Anne didn't live long enough to see her daughter rule, to know her daughter was no queen consort but a queen in her own right.

At least they say Anne was happy in her final hours, that she laughed when she heard Henry brought in an expert swordsman from France for her beheading. "I heard say the executioner was very good, and I have a little neck." She giggled and wrapped her hands around her throat.

To this day, I have no idea how she found the strength to laugh. How could anyone laugh in her place? Amidst the false accusations of incest and tales of her brother's execution, where did she find the strength to waltz to the scaffold in grey damask and ermine fur?

Good Christian people, I am come hither to die, for according to the law, and by the law I am judged to die, and therefore I will speak nothing against it. I am come hither to accuse no man, nor to speak anything of that, whereof I am accused and condemned to die, but I pray God save the king and send him long to reign over you, for a gentler nor a more merciful prince was there never: and to me he was ever a good, a gentle and sovereign lord. And if any person will meddle of my cause, I require them to judge the best. And thus I take my leave of the world and of you all, and I heartily desire you all to pray for me.

She wrote a poem in her cell before she died, but it was no love letter to her husband, no record for her king. In the end, she wanted nothing more than to die, to sleep in peace at last.

O Lord have mercy on me, to God I commend my soul.

1,000,000 Micromorts

… what is this, the heat death of the universe?

What is the deadliest thing you can think of? Drinking liquid nitrogen? Standing next to a nuclear bomb as it explodes? Severing your ribs from your spine and pulling out your lungs? *Excellent choice, that last one. The blood eagle, a ritualized form of execution detailed in late skaldic poetry.*

Technically speaking, we can't say that any of these activities are one million micromorts. *Probably close, but not quite. Maybe someone died of exposure before they died from having no ribs.* One million micromorts is a guaranteed death sentence. No escape whatsoever.

When we are young, we overestimate the gift of life. We live as if we are immortal, because every step feels like a new beginning, and there will be a second chance for everything. When we are old, we underestimate the gift of life. Confined to a withering body and struggling with a fading mind, we can scarcely believe that the goings-on of this world once mattered to us.

In reality, life is not a gift, but a loan. What goes up must come down. The only activity with a risk of one million micromorts is *living*.

We are desperate gamblers, each and every one of us. Mathematically speaking, the odds are not stacked in our favor; at this point, the least we can do to ensure a positive expected value is to make the gain worth the risk. We trust so that there will always be someone waiting for us. We love so that we always have someone to wait for. We chase our dreams so that someday, the world will remember the risks we took and the sacrifices that we made.

"You know that place between sleep and awake, the place where you can still remember dreaming? That's where I'll always love you, Peter Pan. That's where I'll be waiting."

THE UNITED NATION OF POETRY REJECTS
THE FULL STOP
(from *A Series of Punctuation*)

by Hajar Hussaini

---

a full stop is in the tongue's arsenal [a mallet chapandaz keeps] it intervenes in every motion enforcing a sentence, bonds paragraphs through the separation of the varying verbs / then unifies them to co-exist, but in the eyes of the other marks it's a ruthless authoritarian / imposing a constitutional referendum

a portrait of dot is in its entrance / against guernica and the installation of bani adam *every statement needs a full stop* [a speech of] *my source of food is pause, the freedom to talk*, it tosses my stream of consciousness onto the dark cavities of teeth / making me echo what comes through the ear / it gets routine order from the frontal cortex

it conceals sentiments that don't fit into a linear structure, with an amplitude of my rejection fear—the fear of being called out the violent member of the group – and when there's neither a time nor an interest—i swallow them in a ratio of making shorter statements [cubicandtender] not harsh like ashes i passed through

or the goblins of human rights, as an object the terminal period is an ak47 pointed at my dictionary of pouring out, initializing the establishments. My therapist says *this act is post-traumatic* [omittingstress, drinkingfromher cup] and in my mind i commute to a post office where the letters can be sent / like a mailbox i feel emptied

A DISTINCTIVE DUPLICATION
(from *A Series of Punctuation*)

by Hajar Hussaini

Letter *P* is among the sounds that blocks the airflow, it has a coalescence with soft S / or key sounding C and/or L which makes a thing a common english word. Rarely found in Farsi and if so imported by tradesmen like a tin of pringles. For example, there is a sudden release of air that follows an ellipse's *P*. There: clouds are created. I eavesdrop on the friction of two unvoiced rubbing against each other.

Throughout my adolescence I circled words with those three letters. Copied from textbooks and recited them from a blue recycled journal, its front and back covered in the logo of the international children's emergency fund. I drew straight lines on top of zigzagged horizons to create an equal number of squares. In each I carefully placed one word / was a frequent exercise prior to stretching myself on a shared mattress bed.

I was told that my *table of disembodied words is not how learning a language works* but one dissects a complex into its capsules. In an age of modern explosives and extinction of languages, english became my precise measurement of stress. Plosives, in them, was a theatrical movement of my lips: how their natives articulated. Ellipses are continuation. Of three periods.

Cycles of internal bleedings. *Endometriosis*, an Asian American doctor years later diagnosed. *It is making you an infertile woman*. That I, *need to hurry*. I can ignore their placements in prose. In poetry, they are invasive. Intruding a community and removing individuals. Not needed. Not needed. Already implied. As suspension points or for a stuttering effect, ellipses are always together, if one is not fitting in, a writer cannot separate.

MY FICTION: REMEMBERING FIFTY YEARS OF WORK

by Richard Kostelanetz

In memory of Lawrence Sterne (1713-1768)

[PREFACE:]

In the fifty years that I've been writing fiction, I have produced:

1.   a novella with no more than two words to a paragraph (and then, in one of its two published forms, no more than two words to a book page) (*One Night Stood*, 1969, 1977),

2.   a visual fiction whose principal narrative action comes from the addition of the alphabet's letters (*In the Beginning*, 1971),

3.   words printed on syntactically continuous looping plastic strips that lack beginnings or ends (*Infinities-Stories*, 2005),

4.   two books of scrupulously Minimal Fictions that are no more than three words in length, most having only two words or one prior to the period (aka full stop) that necessarily concludes the narrative action—one with several to a page for 80 pages (*Minimal Fictions*, 1993); the other with one fiction to a page for 900 pages (*Micro Stories*, 2010),

5.   stories that develop through a series of shapes that are composed exclusively of letters or words ("Football Forms," 1968; *Come Here*, 1975, respectively),

6.   fictions whose meaning changes with the introduction not of other words but of different configurations of nonverbal imagery ("Obliterate," 1974; *Reincarnations*, 1978),

7.   narratives composed entirely of nonrepresentational line-drawings that metamorphose so systemically that each image in the sequence belongs only to its particular place (several volumes of *Constructivist Fictions*, 1974-1991; *March*, 1990; *CF 1*, 2013; *CF 2*, 2013; *Symmetries*, 2013),

8.   representational graphic narratives composed of square shapes shifting their places within the fields established by successive pages (*Of 4 & 5 Squares*, 2014; *With 6 Squares*, 2014) or chessboard moves (*Checkmates: Eight Narratives*, 2015),

9.   individual sentences that are either the openings or the closings of otherwise unwritten stories (*Openings & Closings*, 1975; *More Openings & Closings*, 2012; *A Book of Openings*, 2012; "Endings," 2018),

10.   "Skeletal Fictions" with horizontal sequences of words, separated by more horizontal space than is customary, without blatant syntactical connectives (but narrative implications in the spacing nonetheless) (c. 1988, collected in *Furtherest Fictions*, 2013),

11.   stories composed of just cut-up photographs whose rectangular chips move systemically, as well as symmetrically, through narrative cycles ("Recall," 1978),

12.   separate modular fictions of photographs that can be read in any order (*Reincarnations*), of words or line-drawings whose positions in a sequence are interchangeable (and thus can be shuffled) (*Rain Rains Rain*, 1975, and *And So Forth*, 1979 respectively), and of sentences that are reordered in systemic ways to produce different emphases of the same words and narrative motifs (*Foreshortenings & Other Stories*, 1978), if not radically different stories,

13. circular stories that flow from point to point over a single page but lack definite beginnings or ends (in *More Short Fictions*, 1980; *Verbal Fictions*, 2012),

14. narratives, some only a page in length but one as long as a book, composed exclusively of numerals (*Exhaustive Parallel Intervals*, 1979; *Seven Jewish Short Fictions*, 2006; *1-99*, 2013),

15. stories composed entirely of words that rhyme with one another—some two words long, others three, most even more populous ("Rhyming," c. 1990, collected in *Furtherest Fictions*, 2013),

16. a fiction composed of sixteen different (but complimentary) narratives interwoven one sentence at a time in print in sixteen different typefaces, on audiotape told one sentence as a time in sixteen purposefully different amplifications of a single voice, and in a performance spoken by sixteen different readers with individually marked parts ("Seductions," 1980, 1981; *A Polygraphic Novel*, 2016),

17. over two thousand single-sentence fictions representing the epiphanies of otherwise unwritten stories ("Epiphanies," since 1979; *Epiphanies*, two vols., 2012),

18. stories composed entirely of words that are anagrams for each other (*Furtherest Fictions*, 2013) or of phrases anagrammatic to each other (*Verbal Fictions*),

19. manuscripts of single-sentence stories that have been offered to periodical editors not to publish *in toto* but as pools from which they may make their own selections that can then be ordered and designed to their particular tastes ("Epiphanies"; "Openings," since the late 1980s; "Complete Stories" in the 1990s, "Fulcra Fictions" after 2005),

20. a sequence of single-sentence stories that, thanks to structural complexities available in English, are each over two hundred words long ("Single-Sentence Stories" in *Prose Pieces*, 1987),

21. fiction books published in such alternative forms as tabloid-sized newsprint books (*Numbers: Poems & Stories*, 1976; *One Night Stood*, 1977), loose-leaf books (whose pages are gathered in an envelope) (*Rain Rains Rain*, 1976; *And So Forth*, 1979), and accordion books that are 4" high and several feet long (*Extrapolate*, *Modulations*, both 1975),

22. one film and a separate videotape whose only imagery is words evoking narratives (*Openings & Closings*, 1976-78; *Video Stories*, 2004),

23. another film with symmetrical abstract fictions (described in #6 above) that metamorphose in systemic sequence (*Constructivist Fictions*, 1976-77),

24. fictions that exist primarily on audiotape—that cannot be performed live, whose printed version is no more than a score for its realization (*Ululation–An Acoustic Fiction*, 1992),

25. paragraph-long narratives whose successive sentences either add a word to or subtract a word from their immediate predecessors ("Plus/Minus," 1980),

26. fictions whose narrative action comes from long words that are split apart to become other shorter words or adding letters to short words to change with each extra digit their semantic thrust ("Recircuits," "Reroutings," c. 1990),

27. simultaneous translations, initially into Chinese, of single-word fictions and, initially into Spanish, of single-sentence fictions that are published on the same page as the English originals (*Simultaneous Translations*, 2008) or appear in the same place on a video screen ("1001 Stories," in *Action! Yes*, 2010),

28. translations into English of the historic single-sentence fictions of Ramón Gómez de la Serna and Francis Fénéon, writing initially in Spanish and French respectively, both of whose minimal texts were badly or insufficiently translated previously ("Kosti's Versions," *forthcoming*),

29. a linear narrative whose single-scene paragraphs are no more than two words in length ("Milestones in a Life," 1970),

30. a novel-length fiction compressed solely into the form of a family tree ("On Fortune and Fate," 1969),

31. two books of "conceptual" fictions, one a novel, the other a collection of stories, in which thick spine-bound collections of evenly cut blank pages are prefaced by a cover with a resonant title and subtitle ("Constructivist"), along with a single-page preface that establish a context for what follows (*Tabula Rasa, Inexistences,* 1978),

32. reimaging myself inside or beside an historical figure ("Leonardo & Me," 1998),

33. one book of and about *Conceptual Fictions* (2012),

34. another book exemplifying the conceptual ideal of resonant absence (Richard Kostelanetz's Loves and Lives, 2013),

35. "Overlapped Minimal Fictions" (1993) in which one continuous stream of letters contains three words, each of which incorporates at its ends at least the two opening letters of its successor or at its beginning at least the concluding two letters of its predecessor,

36. a cycle of one hundred and twenty-seven erotic stories, each successively one word longer than its immediate predecessor until, at the sixty-four-word length, each new story becomes one word shorter than its immediate predecessor ("More or Less," c. 1980),

37. *Two-Element Stories* (2003) and *Three-Element Stories* (1998) that depend upon a period (aka a "full stop") to make the implicitly preceding disconnected words become a skeletal narrative,

38. a *Condensed Novel* (2008) whose fourteen chapters are each a single sentence long,

39. *Contagion* (2003), a narrative fifty feet long on clear acetate,

40. *Running Headers* (2015) and *Running Footers* (2015) weave fiction(s) wholly in the headings of otherwise blank pages,

41. a visual fiction five times higher than it is wide ("The True Adventures of Don Juan," 2012),

42. *99 Video Stories* whose sequence is randomized, to exploit a capability unavailable in spine-bound print (c. 2010),

43. "Micro Novels" and "Micro Novellas" that resemble each other in brief length but differ as genres by range and number of words,

44. *Fict/ions* and "Fulcra Fictions" that depend upon discovering within a single word two shorter words that, concluding with a period, make a narrative,

45. *GhoStories* (2012), a book where within one long word is boldfaced a shorter word so that the two suggest a narrative,

46. *One-Letter Changes* (2013), another book in which a narrative results from placing beside one word a second (and sometimes a third and forth) differing from its predecessor in the change of only a single letter,

47. single words meant to suggest movement from here to elsewhere, which is to say narrative (*Monoepics*, 2013).

48. *Homophones* (2013) whose narratives result from positioning next to each other two words that sound alike even if spelled differently,

49. short narratives whose forward movement results from the reader's turning over the book's pages (*Page Turners*, 2014),

50. *A to Z: Four Novellas* (2015), which consists of four alphabets, each successor in an increasingly more obscure typeface,

51. *Love: A Narrative* (2016) has only that word suggesting a narrative by becoming smaller and larger on only recto pages,

52. *Enfoldings* (2016) are very short descriptions so fantastic that they are necessarily fictional,

53. "Truncated" fictions consisting of single-sentence "episodes" that do not obviously follow from each other (*Furtherest Fictions*, 2013),

54. "Discontinuous Stories" from which many possibly connecting words are missing (*Further Furtherest Fictions*, 2018),

55. infinite narratives composed by writing on each side of a card individual words that lead into each other (*To&-Fro&* (2013),

56. *Unscience Fictions* (2014) that move beyond known possibilities, both above and below,

57. several volumes of pristine erotica describing seduction without employing "dirty words" or explicit descriptions (*Erotic Minimal Fictions*, 2012: *Him & Her*, 2013; *Lovings: A Book of Stories*, 2015: A Polygraphic Novel; Translovings: A Collection of Stories, 2016; Excelsior, 2017; Amen, 2017),

58. stories that fold into themselves, rather than going somewhere (*Enfoldings* 2016),

59. a four-hour film composed of verbal and visual *Epiphanies* that have no connection to each other, either vertically or horizontally, other than common fictional structure (1981-93),

60. videotapes whose abstract visual syntheses become an accompanying counterpoint to the more concrete audio narration (*Seductions/Relationships*, 1987; *Secret Stories*, 2004),

61. rewritings of classic stories to make them contemporary and personal ("Kosty the Ghostwriter," 2010; *Kosti's Pep Dream*, 2013; *American Writing*, 2018),

62. reinterpretations of a certain mode of visual art that I establish by putting within a picture frame only my words (*Narrative Pictures*, 2015),

63. *Epitaphs* (2016) pictures of gravestones whose fictional inscriptions portray lives of various sorts,

64. book-length narratives about the process of writing such a narrative, each with only one word to a page (*Writing a Novel*, 2016; *Writing Another Novel*, 2016; *Rewriting a Novel*, 2017),

65. an erotic memoir consisting only of typographically daunting first names whose common theme is ambiguous gender (*Kosti's Lovers*, 2018),

66. a narrative with implicit greater distances between the sentences that thus appear singly on each book page (*An Episodic Novel*, 2015),

67. a book-length narrative with several chapters, each marked by its own style of typogarbage, incidentally realizing a Mikhail Bahktin ideal impossible in the mid-20th Century (*A Polyphonic Novel*, 2016),

68. a novel-length narrative whose chapters consist solely of roman numerals consecutively only on recto pages (*100 Chapters: A Novel*, 2016),

69. an extended exploration of erotic experience with narrators who are not straight males (*Translovings: A Collection of Stories*, 2016),

70. brief narratives composed only from the source word that introduces it and thus becomes its title (*Parthogenesis*, 2020),

71. a single continuous line of typogarbage that runs over 100 pages (*A Mononarrative*, 2019),

72. book-length abstract graphic narratives that differ from more familiar "graphic novels" (aka higher comics) as nonrepresentational images metamorphose over successive pages (*Modulations and Extrapolate*, both 1975, and *Symmetries*, 2013),

73. an ebook in which the reader is invited to choose his or her own typeface and size for reading them (*More Micro Stories*, 2017),

74. minimal science fictions, evoking alternative world(s) with only a few words to a sentence (*Ficciones*, 2017),

75. a book with several stories running horizontally and nonsynchronously atop each other over successive pages (*Unscience Fictions*, 2015),

76. linear narratives that depend upon the same word(s) being progressively enlarged or, less frequently, reduced only on successive recto pages (*Joy*, 2015; *Presence*, 2016),

77. reframing a classic fiction with the addition of my own complimentary text (*The Death and Redeath of Ivan Ilyitch*, 2016),

78. FlipBook & Flipbook (2016). These revive an old form approximating a pre-film narrative (sometimes called a Zoetrope), but here only letters change in the same place on successive pages, creating new words on every recto. The second book has the same text with a smaller format, the two books again exploring how the same materials, here only words typically, can seem different if they appear in radically different formats,

79. <---> (2016) contains two-word narratives that can be read in either direction from the edges of a two-page spread,

80. single English words that, when typeset into a continuous circle, contain other shorter words that compliment their host in suggesting a narrative (*Ouroborostories*, 2018),

81. probably a few other departures whose character cannot yet, for better or worse, be neatly encapsulated (???),

82. not just no juvenilia, though in college I outlined a novel echoing Nat West's *A Day of the Locust*; but no conventional fiction–absolutely none–which is to say nothing that could pass a university course/workshop in "fiction writing" (and perhaps get me a job teaching such), and thus no familiar milestone from which simple-minded critics could then measure "development,"

83. the purest *oeuvre* of fiction as fiction–in the great tradition of Cervantes, Sterne, and Chekhov, scarcely autobiographical, scarcely compromised by vulgar considerations–that anyone has ever done.

These fictions of mine have appeared in over fifty literary magazines, while over a dozen volumes of these fictions have appeared in print (and my critical essays were collected as *The Old Fictions and the New*, 1987). Entries on me featuring my fiction appear in both the *Merriam-Webster Encyclopedia of Literature* (1995) and *A Reader's Guide to 20th Century Writers* (Oxford, 1995). Nonetheless, reviews of individual books have been few, and neither commercial contracts for this work nor grants for fiction writing have come my way. No institution has ever asked me to teach a "fiction workshop." Only one story was ever anthologized by someone else (Eugene Wildman, in his *Experiments in Prose*, back in 1969).

Would "a line of milk bottles of a bodega shelf constitute fiction," the fiction critic Jerome Klinkowitz asked of an earlier draft of this memoir? Yes, if they contained different amounts, because any explanation of how they got that way would necessarily be a narrative.

In my fiction as in my poetry, I've tried to be "the most inventive ever," certainly in America, and probably have succeeded with an ambition cultivated by a few. At minimum, may I think I've expanded the world of fiction writing, establishing new turfs that others will cultivate, no doubt in different ways.

OVERSOUL
The Poet Policeman Of Lambshire

(excerpts)

by P. S. Lutz

[Note: To find the complete adventures of The Poet Police-
man, you can visit our website. Below, enjoy some selected,
non-consecutive scenes in print!]

News from Britannia:

Who? Otto and Zoe Philia. *What?* Are separated. *Where?* Lambshire or some shire
near there. *When?* Hopefully not forever
because we love them much more together
than apart. *Why?* His career comes first
and nothing comes between her and her
dog. *How?* Love is so inscrewtable.

Word of the day: *Dover sole - n. a de-*
licious species of flatfish in the family
Soleidae
#1 Band: *Generatalia*
#1 Song: *My My Generatalia by Generata-*
lia
#1 Number: *One*
#1 Color: *A tie between Orange and Pump-*
kin
#1 Food: *Fish and Chips*
#1 Bestseller: *Generatalia—Their DIY Mu-*
sical Moment that Changed the World
#1 Dog: *Zoe Philia's Rugo*
#1 Blog: *News from Britannia*

Unlikely and unsettling as the heralded morning news might have sounded to him, Daed Oversoul weathered existence another day and wondered what would become of the English language he so loved and had so for so long. The end of words seemed to have been coming for some time, but not merely as a vain promise from academics who study vital lingual drop-offs and trendy verbal

stowaways for a living; it was more of a premonitory sense in Daed that silence could somehow be forced upon humanity, that even the word *silence* could somehow be stolen, lifted quietly from the collective tongue, bought and sold.

English, unbeknownst hitherto to the entire planet, was owned as it had always been by one British family, the Words. Lord Frisbee Word II, who preferred the title Lord Byword as a sort of elitist play on words, may or may not have had a recent stroke, but most assuredly and recently announced that he was to put his family's singular, ancient, prized possession and heirloom up for auction, one word at a time. The notion that one of the populace could now collect royalties upon overhearing his or her newly purchased word (or words) bandied about in common street chatter made for a mob mentality the likes of which had never before threatened the staid, secular sanctity of the auction house.

In immiscible human matters of this rare sort, not to be mixed or sifted without singular sensitivity of intellect, Daed Oversoul was often and eagerly sought by police and high-ranking officials of the Anglican sovereignty. Professionally, Daed was a poet, the British Isles having claimed him as their laureled own on one of his coffee-house, pub, and church tours just before the new millennium. Now almost twenty years later, now a full-time poet laureate and part-time crime liaison, Daed Oversoul stood at the lofty Word family's front door and awaited entrance and further acquaintance with Lord Frisbee Byword's world-shaking decision to sell off the noble, primogenial English lexicon.

"What gives you the right to question me in my personal or professional comportment, young man?" asked Lord Word II quite civilly over tea.

Daed sipped and nodded respectfully. "I understand your concern over my unofficial position in this investigation, Sir Frisbee, but, as someone of your lexicographical stature can appreciate, the police favor a man or woman of letters over one of facts and figures in matters of this nature."

"Matters of this nature?" stickled Frisbee the Lord of the Words. "I ask, has there ever been a matter of this nature before?"

Daed puzzled and sipped over the question. "No. I think this rivals the potential sale of an ocean or even a star."

"A star, you say? Are the stars not for sale?"

That uncomfortable consideration just then entered Daed's mind. "No. I don't believe they are. Are they?"

"Of course they're not for sale, my boy," averred Sir Frisbee. "You can't eat a star, can you?" Daed smiled faintly, shook his head obligingly. "No, and you can't drink a star and, if you can't eat it or drink it, young man, then why on earth would you dare desire it?"

Daed reflected to himself as he took another sip of tea, thought about the many priceless treasures of his life, all of which could not be practically (or legally in the case of some) eaten or drunk. "After all these devout years, have you begun to question the value of words, Lord Word? Numbers and letters have long been jostling for predominance in the world, but words will surely win out over formulas in the end."

Lord Frisbee Byword rose to his feet unceremoniously. "Is that your lettered opinion, poet policeman?"

"It is," said Daed as he stood and bowed his head only slightly in obeisance.

"Young man, I have an offer for you."

"Yes, Lord Word? Lord Byword?"

Then tossed Sir Frisbee, "I will sell you your own name, both names in fact—a two-for-one as the Americans say: *Daedal* and *Oversoul* for ten thousand pounds. Take it or leave it, but do for a moment envisage yourself earning a wholesome, fulsome income, not by piddly poems mind you, but by the mere mention of your given name. Daedal. Oversoul. There, if you had already purchased those two precious words from me, I would now and with every forthcoming greeting in your company be in your debt. But, alas, you are a man of letters, not a man of facts and figures, and as such will indubitably refuse participation in this private business venture and for that lack of economic foresight, Mr. Daedal Oversoul, I must bid you, good day."

Daed walked back to the Lambshire police station with no good news for its chief. "Sorry to say, sir, but Lord Frisbee Byword is not the steward of the English language that his long and faithful lineage had to have entrusted him to be."

"Is that it, Oversoul?" chided the chief. "We've come to expect more from you than this. Any one of my men and, if I'm honest, my women, too, can and will almost always come back with head in hand, tail between the legs. You can't tell me that on the same day we discover that the Queen's English does not belong to her or the crown or to all of us, but to some codger of a soul named Lord Frisbee Byword, we also just happen to discover that we may have lost it utterly, every last word to the great abyss and wind along with our God-given ability to reason." Daed shouldered suddenly the full weight of twenty-six letters on the wild wind. The Lambshire police chief could not and did not relent, "You're a bloody laureate poet, Oversoul; don't tell me you're giving up before there's rhyme and reason to this crime of the ages against humanity."

"No. I won't, Chief," assured Daed, although he didn't quite know what he meant in his declaration not to give up on the challenge of convincing Lord Frisbee Byword that language, like a star, is something ill-fit for the mortal marketplace. He thought to himself that Sir Frisbee's own logic could be applied in a formal rebuttal, that of words not being suitable to eat or drink and, therefore, purposefully owned by no one. Yes, no one should own the English language, not even its rightful owner by birthright, Lord Frisbee Word II.

***

News from Americana:

Who? Poplar Tart AKA Pop Tart. *What?* She's single again. *Where?* C'mon, the girl's a global sensation. *When?* Probably not for long, 'cause she's pipin'. *Why?* She's young and free and doesn't want to settle down until she's twenty-one. *How?* Someone said something she really didn't like.

Word of the day: *loverroll - n. a full 360° couple rotation during genital or oral sex*
#1 Band: *Pop Tart*
#1 Song: *Eat Me for Breakfast by Pop Tart*

```
#1 Number: Two
#2 Band: Generatalia
#2 Song: My My Generatalia by Generatalia
#1 Food: Pop Tart
#1 Sport: Ultimate Frisbee
#1 Blog: News from Americana
```

News of the young and famous socialite Zoe Philia's arrest near a shire near Lambshire was upstaged by Lord Frisbee Byword's formal press-release announcement that he was indeed beginning the process of transferring nearly half a million English words from the storehouse of the Word Family Library to the Lambshire Auctioneers Society. Word stock came into existence and went up in the very same moment, with predictions from economic experts that words were to become the next great natural resource on the planet. Other nations would have certainly followed suit and flooded the marketplace with a polyglot promise of booming international economy, a fiscal flow of loquacious millions, except for the fact that only England could boast particular, legal ownership of its native language. Word stock shot up even farther on the grounds of this new natural resource being classified as a limited and exhaustible, distinctively English one.

Daed Oversoul the poet knew the ineffable value of words and continued to regard them pricelessly so, despite the world's late attempt to monetize eloquence. The marketplace value of his own two names, he thought, could not have been set less accurately by their owner, Lord Frisbee Byword. *Daedal* and *oversoul*, in vulgar terms, were no less than million-dollar words each, just like all the others, even *the*, *and*, *so*, and *but*. English like all other languages, however, was not vulgar in the least, but noble. The acknowledgment that someone could soon potentially hijack Daed's given name and then force him to pay perpetual ransom for its use in speech and writing roiled Daed's soul. "I am going to make Lord Frisbee Byword eat his words," said Daed just loud enough to himself to be convinced of the indefatigable power of the spoken word.

Sir Frisbee sat on his settee for tea and engaged his mind and digits in a unique new word game that came to him by pure surprise in the post. English letters poured out of the package onto the coffee table in a random design that no wordsmith or man named Word could resist intelligibly arranging. The uniqueness of the game was not the mere assortment of bold, stray letters, but that the letters themselves were edible biscuits, rather perfect with tea. The note from Daedal Oversoul to Lord Frisbee Word II read: *Before you eat these words of yours, read them over and over again aloud until your hunger for their recantation overtakes your senses.*

The first order of this playful business was to solve the baked, fifteen-letter, alphabetical puzzle and Sir Frisbee giddily invoked his ancient lineage's eye for lexical detail to decipher quickly the *them* in the phrase. The rest came facilely from his evolved word-game skill set as much as from Lord Frisbee Byword's memory of the recent comment he made to the press: *Let them eat words.* "Let them eat words. Let them eat words. Let them eat words," Sir Frisbee repeated in honor of Daed Oversoul's request, but no remorse or wish to recant his infamous comment pricked the old man's conscience. He ate the fifteen little letter biscuits anyway and toasted Daed's inventive method of persuasion with a raised teacup, "Here's to the word *biscuit* and the word *tea*; may no one purchase them today, Daedal Oversoul. Good try, my boy, but you must bake many more letters and make much haste."

A letter came to Daed's address and he, the man of letters, sat down with it, anticipating neutral to discouraging news, definitely not good news from the Word estate. Lord Frisbee Byword's handwriting was breathtakingly beautiful to Daed and his romantic nature, evidence alone that there was still hope for the English language and its safe prospective keeping outside the walls of the Lambshire auction house and the reach of world industry captains. He wrote:

My Dear Daedal,

You must send my cook your recipe for comestible English alphabet biscuits. They hit the proverbial spot, that abyssal domain between nourishment and insatiable craving. Must I be cookie-quoted again by you, clever boy, or will you perchance send me an edible poem of yours? I would fain consider recompensing you for the privilege of eating your words. Who will buy your name, Daedal Oversoul, if not you? My offer stands, though I, sadly, am mostly found sitting out my remaining days.

Cheers,
Frisbee

It was somewhat less than good news, but more than neutral was the spirit of their correspondence, these two men of words with ample decent words between them. Daed set Sir Frisbee's letter down on his desk, got up, stepped into his tiny flat's galley kitchen, and began to create a new, experimental form of poetry.

My words to you are free, Sir Frisbee. Why must yours come at such a cost? May this puzzle poem nourish you, body, mind, and spirit. One word should do the bidding. Lord Frisbee Byword eagerly spilled the alphabetical contents of Daed's padded envelope parcel to him and began to reconstruct the po-

et's mind on his coffee table, nibbling on crumbs the baked-good letters had left behind in postal transit and just then again when they all landed in front of him. "What are you intimating here, my boy?" said Sir Frisbee to the twenty-nine biscuits. "The 'F' is clearly the only capitalized one of the lot. One word, you say?" His hands went furiously to task upon the sweet, lettered mound. "Do I know this word?" The word began to take elongated shape beneath deft, spindling fingers. "I am Lord Frisbee Byword, so, yes, I know *Floccinaucinihilipilification* as if it were one of my own children. And do I not now know you, Daedal Oversoul, as if you were my own son?" Sir Frisbee then shed a tear as rare as *Floccinaucinihilipilification* to the English speakers' eye. "Do I know what it means, my boy? I do indeed, Daedal: *The act of regarding something as unimportant*. Is this your new name for me? Floccinaucinihilipilification? If so, I accept it and its meaning as a knighthood. I am the act incarnate of regarding something as unimportant. Thank you, son, for my new title and life calling."

***

News from Easteria:

Who? Winnay Le Poux. *What*? He's a shocking romantic partner of a famous person. *Where*? On the reality television show, Shocking Romantic Partners of Famous People. *When*? Weekly and streaming all the time. *Why*? Love is a many-splintered thing. *How*? No one really knows, but Winnay says that his long-term relationship with his movie-star girlfriend, Hissy Fit, is based mostly on mutual disrespect.

Word of the day: *roversole - n. a wandering flatfish or a walking shoe for a dog*
#1 Band: *Dear John and Jane Doe*
#1 Song: *Nice Rack by Dear John and Jane Doe*
#2 Song: *Hum Hum Humbuckin' by Tel and Strat*
#3 Song: *Wipe Your Boca by Kleenexa and Baby Wype*
#4 Song: *Buck Naked by Dear John and Jane Doe*
#5 Song: *Eat Me for Breakfast by Pop Tart*
#1 Number: *Six*
#6 Song: *My My Generatalia by Generatalia*

#1 Television Show: *Shocking Romantic Partners of Famous People*
#1 Blog: *News from Easteria*

En route to a surprise second visit to the Word Manor, Daed stopped off at the Lambshire Auctioneers Society after having spoken with Truth Bertholdt, the auction house curator and liaison. He hoped a sit-down in her office would help him amply understand how nearly five hundred thousand English words were to be gathered up and then systematically disseminated to all corners of the globe for a bid price. "How does it work Ms. Bertholdt, may I ask? Will the words come to you as a computer file or are they more like discrete works of art, calligraphic prints on card stock paper that you sell one at a time from an easel?" Daed then imagined a winner walking away from the auction with an 8 ½ x 11 print of an invaluable, eximious term like *paregmenon* or *sesquipedalian* or *eximious* for that matter, transporting it home ever so carefully, displaying it proudly on his or her mantle, then waiting like a spider in its web for someone, anyone to dare speak out or write down this newly acquired intellectual property, and then at last lowering the fangs of predatory profit upon the unwitting word consumer. "And will each of the new owners of the English language be known to us newfound consumers of speech after the auction concludes? And do you think every word will be sold? And..."

"Yah, zat is a lot of questions," Truth Bertholdt expressed, mostly to halt the onslaught, her German accent reminding Daed just how far-reaching English and so many other languages had become in the post-modern world.

"Forgive me, Ms. Bertholdt, but this matter has a life-and-death feel to it for me."

She smiled cursory understanding and proceeded to answer Daed's questions in the order that they were posed, "'How does it work?' Zat is a good question. I don't know exactly, Mr. Oversoul."

"Please call me Daed."

Truth nodded. "Yah, Daed, I don't know how zis little Lambshire auction house can be expected to hold so many words as zat and so many bidders, unless it is done virtually like everything else zese days. Zere will likely be no formal prints of za words, but zere will be receipts and, zerefore, za new owner or owners of za English language will be known publicly to all za native and non-native English speakers."

"And writers."

"Yah, and writers," she concurred with a respectful, succinct nod and smile, then continued, "Your last question: Do I zink all of za words will be sold? Yah, I do zink zat, but I don't know zat zey will be purchased by more zan one person."

Daed mused on Truth's speculation. "A whole legal transfer from one owner to another – the forest, not the trees." he said sotto voce.

Truth overheard Daed and commented, "Maybe Lord Frisbee Word II will buy his own words, just to let everyone know how valuable words really are, how special language is for all of us."

"A compelling theory, Truth," said Daed.

"Yah, but I didn't give you permission to call me by my first name."

"Oh, I'm sorry for that," Daed immediately replied, hung his head slightly, politely. Truth smiled then laughed.

"It was a joke, yah? You are free to call me Truth, Daed, at least until someone starts bidding on my name."

Daed was relieved not to have misread Truth. "Would you bid on your name if the Lambshire Auctioneers Society allowed their employees to do so?"

Truth did not think too long on the notion, "No. I already own my name, Daed, as I'm certain you do as well, mine and yours."

Ownership of one's own name was not as strange a concept to him before Daed Oversoul met Lord Frisbee Byword. Self-possession was a virtue, lauded by many peoples, by many nations. If Daed already owned Truth as she seemed to suggest, then how could somebody possibly buy the words *daedal* and *oversoul* at the Lambshire auction house and have it that anything at all in Daed's life would change? Was he making this prospective sale of the English language more about his own assaulted sensibility than about Sir Frisbee's motives, whatever they truly were? Was he making more of the sociolexicological issue than it was worth? Was all of it a waste of his personal and police time? A hoax?

"Is all of this just a hoax?" perseverated in Daed's head as he waited for the Word mansion's elevated front door to open to him again, for Lord Frisbee Byword to appear and field this direct question and, once and for all, come clean on the matters of English potentially becoming a second-class language product. No such hopeful, fruitful dialogue ensued, however, since Sir Frisbee was not at home and Chief Noble of the Lambshire police department had just rolled up onto the Word Manor pebble driveway in a squad car.

"Oversoul!" the chief bellowed as he rolled down his driver-side window. Daed turned and acknowledged his friend and employer with a wave and a smile. "You're bloody under arrest!"

"I'm what, Chief?"

"You heard me, Oversoul. Get in and let's sort this unpleasantness out together." Daed stood his ground at the Words' main entrance.

"What unpleasantness is that, Chief?"

Chief Noble sat his ground within his vehicle, "The unpleasantness of Otto Philia's death, that's what unpleasantness."

"Really?" Daed bewailed as he walked toward the parked police car.

"Really," echoed the chief. "C.C., our new coroner, hasn't yet determined if it was choking or poisoning, or both, but Otto Philia apparently ate his own name in biscuit letters and it's unofficially a case of either inadvertent auto-asphyxiation or auto-poisoning by the edible word *Otto*." Daed was bewildered in a momentary Bewusstseinslage as he got into the passenger side front seat. "You were the last one to see Otto alive and you recently showed a fancy for his wife, and you have been on quite a baking binge of late, Oversoul. What do have to say for yourself?"

"I own you, Chief Noble, and you own me."

"Have you lost your wits, Oversoul? Words have been known to drive some men of letters over the deep end."

Daed rephrased, "I think I know what Lord Frisbee Byword is doing."

"Do you now? Do you know what you're doing?"

"I do, Chief," Daed assured. "Right now, I'm going to buy some time in one of your jail cells and tomorrow I'm going to figure out how to buy back the English language."

The chief gainsays, "Buy it back? Is that to say that you at one time owned English outright, Oversoul?"

Daed nodded. "It does, I did, and I will indeed again."

"I'll take your word for it and, on my father's good name, we will sort you out, this unpleasant business of you and the Otto Philia murder charge," commanded the chief. He then offered Daed one of his alphabet biscuits from an open bakery bag. "I don't know about eating whole words, Oversoul, but these individual, assorted letters go down pretty easy." Daed graciously took a baked 'n' and as the sweet, buttery savor alighted onto his tongue, he imagined that he was eating the word *nobility*, taking it back home to his body and soul.

***

News from Borealia:

Who? Otto Philia. *What?* Is dead. *Where?* A shire somewhere near Lambshire. *When?* Really recently. *Why?* Nobody knows. Who would kill the guy who coined the expression What up, Canine? *How?* Half homicide and half suicide but all Otto Philia all the way until the final credits. Daed Oversoul has been arrested; Lord Frisbee Byword is missing; Zoe Philia was briefly mentioned as having the best chiality, whatever that means, and is now reunited with her dog Rugo.

Word of the day: *cloverknoll - n. a hill of clover; a really lucky discovery*
#1 Band: *Generatalia*
#1 Song: *Take a Really Really Really Long Look at Me by Generatalia*
#2 Song: *Sticky Love by Ban Daid*
#3 Song: *Nice Rack by Dear John and Jane Doe*
#4 Song: *Buck Naked by Dear John and Jane Doe*
#5 Song: *Hum Hum Humbuckin' by Tel and Strat*
#6 Song: *Wipe Your Boca by Kleenexa and*

Baby Wype
```
#7 Song: Eat Me for Breakfast by Pop Tart
#1 Numbers: One and Eight
#8 Song: My My Generatalia by Generatalia
#1 Natural Phenomenon: Aurora Borealis
#1 Blog: News from Borealia
```

"Bloody hell, bollocks, and bramble fire, Oversoul!" exclaimed Chief Noble of late Lambshire constabulary fame as he approached Daed's jail cell in the morning light. "You used to be an honorary policeman. Is there such a thing as an honorary criminal?"

"Alleged honorary criminal." Daed stood up from his cell cot and joined the chief, bellied up to the bars. "I believe there are honorable criminals and I would hope to be counted among them, if I were one, Chief, but you know that felony is not my bailiwick, especially murder. I've always been more of a pen-and-paper policeman, you know that."

The chief shook his head in dismay. "What about the poison biscuits, Oversoul, and the fact that three out of four letters in Otto's name were the exact same recipe as yours, all but the capital 'O'?"

Daed puzzled over the numbers and baked letters, "Three out of four, Chief?"

"That's right."

"Then we most likely can eliminate Sir Frisbee as a suspect."

"How is that, Oversoul?"

Daed explained, "I baked *Floccinaucinihilipilification* for Lord Word after having baked *Let them eat words* for him. The fifteen biscuit letters of *Let them eat words* surely would have already been eaten by the time *Floccinaucinihilipilification* arrived in the post. And even if the small 't's and the 'o' from *Let them eat words* had been given as a father-in-law's secondhand gift to his daughter's husband, they would have been stale, Chief, found inedible, non-food-like, even to Otto's primitive palate. We are then left with only one 't' and two lower case 'o's from *Floccinaucinihilipilification* and that would not make for the three out of four biscuit letters found whole in Otto Philia's stomach and esophagus. It only accounts for two out of four. Don't you see, Chief?"

The chief shook his head again, but this time in confusion. "Bloody hell, Oversoul, that's a lot of letters for this early hour."

"Forty-four," Daed confirmed to further his argument.

"Well," detoured the chief, "unless our old friend Sir Frisbee has abducted himself, he's no longer a suspect in this case. He's become a missing person and I could use your help to find him, Oversoul."

Daed is taken aback and even steps back a bit from the cell bars. "What? I'm still a suspect in this case, aren't I? Are you asking me to investigate from a jail cell, Chief?"

Chief Noble answered twice with one word: "Yes."

Daed took his turn, shook his head in dismay and confusion, sighed, said, "I'm on it as ever, but I'll need some weapons and some stamps, some sealing wax."

"Anything for the pen-and-paper policeman, Oversoul."

Dear Madam Queen,

I hope this missive finds you in hale health and good spirit. As you may well be apprised, the English language runs the risk of being lost to us English speakers and writers as a free form of expression. Its owner and age-old steward, Lord Frisbee Word II, has gone missing and I fear that the fate of our beloved, ancient, living lexicon may now be in the hands of those who intend to sell it on the black market, well outside the rubric and bounds of the Lambshire Auctioneers Society.

As laureate poet of this sovereign nation, I wish to become proxy steward of the English language in Lord Word's absence. May I have your permission to seek sole ownership of its near half million words and, thus, safeguard their freedom? If this formal request to purchase English from likely non-native-speaking pirates of elocution and composition is acceptable to you, may I also request to borrow seven million pounds? Thank you for your possible assistance in this matter, your queenly discretion, and your potential dispatch.

Sincerely,
Daedal Oversoul

Dear Dear Dear Daedal,

Your words are to me as an alarm and a chiming clock, not the cuckoo sort as many here in the royal court have deemed them. With regard to your request for financial assistance from the crown, none can be lent, I'm afraid. It's not that we British royals haven't the means to reclaim your precious English, it's that we tend not to purchase anything that we can't eat or drink and we almost always steer from lending financial aid to those we judge already rich in spirit. You, Daedal Oversoul, are rich in the immaterial ways. Becoming England's poet laureate is tantamount to taking a holy vow of poverty and forsaking the riches of the world. Three words, beloved poet: Fame without fortune. Good luck with your quest, knight of the Great Isles. Oh, but have I made you a knight? If not, we can certainly arrange a virtual dubbing when all of this English language business is behind us.

Toodle-oo,
  Queen – E

Not to be discouraged in the least by this personal rejection from the queen, when it was once quite customary for Daed Oversoul to receive innumerable rejection letters from literary agents and booking agents and travel agents in the years that led up to his surprise appointment as poet laureate. It was another letter from the queen on that occasion that forged Daed's original sense that she would be willing to do anything for him, whenever he might simply ask:

My dear Daedal Oversoul,

Your poems do for me what snow does for a mountain top, what rain does for a reservoir, what silence does for a sanctuary, what cheese does for a diet—they work wonders. For this, I am pleased to appoint you as poet laureate of England and its isles. Ask anything of me, dear poet, and it shall be yours.

Toodle-oo,
  Queen – E

Daed was now convinced that the only other person in England or anywhere else in the world who could help him in his poor poet's plight, on his desperate, knight-like quest was the only other Word and word owner besides Lord Frisbee Byword, Zoe, his only daughter. She appeared just behind her wafting scent and her lilting tone as she hastened toward him, recited his name, beckoned Daed to his feet in greeting, "Zoe!"

"Daed! Daed! Daed! I know it's only been a week, but I couldn't have survived a fortnight without seeing you again."

Daed's eyes concurred with Zoe's remark and he included his nose and his ears in Zoe's and his shared sense that a fortnight would be entirely too long without reasonable lovers' access. "May I kiss you here, now for the first time or will that build for you a case against me in the murder of your husband and the disappearance of your father?" Zoe just let her lips do the talking, although her tongue quickly joined the tacit but long-winded, loving exchange. The cell bars were conspicuous obstacles to a more carnal expression of feeling and they were also pressing against Zoe and Daed's bodies at particular erogenous-zone points; that sensual happenstance along with the fact that both could claim a wildly adventurous imagination made it that the two were making nothing less than love with one other in the moment. Conversation that required words and some traceable distance between the speaker and the listener's mouths would have to wait for a while, maybe even a week or a fortnight for Daed and Zoe to return from this latest prison fantasy of theirs.

***

News from Britannia: The #1 Blog

Who? Zoe Word. *What?* Is now a widow and is now missing like her father, Lord Frisbee Word II. *Where?* Lambshire or some shire somewhere near there. *When?* Way too soon after the tragedy of losing her superstar, movie-star husband, Otto Philia. *Why?* Nobody really knows why anybody would want to make a widow or a missing person out of anyone. *How?* Life is so mistifying.

Word of the day: *norecord – n. a rare life moment that isn't photographed or videoed*
#1 Band: *Ein Steinway*
#1 Song: *Me and the Keys by Ein Steinway*

#2 Song: *Take a Really Really Really Long Look at Me by Generatalia*
#3 Song: *Sticky Love by Ban Daid*
#4 Song: *Buck Naked by Dear John and Jane Doe*
#5 Song: *Hum Hum Humbuckin' by Tel and Strat*
#6 Song: *Wipe Your Boca by Kleenexa and Baby Wype*
#7 Song: *Nice Rack by Dear John and Jane Doe*
#8 Song: *Eat Me for Breakfast by Pop Tart*
#1 Numbers: *Two and Nine*
#9 Song: *My My Generatalia by Generatalia*
#1 Movie: *Bloody Time Share starring Otto Philia*
#1 Drink: *Bloody Time Share (named after the movie)*

Dear Lambshire Constabulary Chief Noble,

Please be so kind as to manumit mine and England's laureate poet, Daed Oversoul, loose him from his dungeon chains. This unjust incarceration of one of such liberated mind seems to have led only to his loss of grip on the sacred notion of a wealthy spirit. If the poets of the world are no longer able to grasp the concept that there isn't enough green for everyone's grass or garden, then civilization as we know it will most assuredly collapse. We can't have that, now can we? Set the poor poet free and pin the crime on someone else as what must be done in desperate times to preserve peace, class, and crown.

Toodle-oo,

Queen – E

Chief Noble read the letter aloud to Daed and, with a patriotic, welling eye, he freed his friend and honorary policeman from jail. "I'm going to miss you, Oversoul. You brought some class and culture to the cell block and you never once complained about the grub, the pitifully plain viands of the British penal system."

"I'm not going anywhere, Chief," said Daed plainly. "We'll probably be seeing each other more than ever now." He then pressed, "Have you any new leads on Zoe or Sir Frisbee?"

"None, I'm afraid, but there is this lad with the adhesive bandages."

"Which lad is that?"

The chief indoctrinated Daed in the activist ways of Ban Daid, the K-Pop/Celtic singer, "We've slapped him with tickets and fines for his activism, but he just keeps sticking his adhesive bandages anywhere he likes. He said to me, 'The planet is bleeding and Ban Daid is not just like putting adhesive bandages on the busted soul of humanity, he's like saving the world with music and like medicine.'"

Daed appealed for clarity, "Did he really refer to himself in the third person?"

"That he did," clarified the chief. "And he's not a humble-pie type of bloke, is he?"

Daed's head lowered in thought, he suggested, "I think we should follow Ban Daid, Chief, see if there's any truth to his claim about the bleeding planet and these medicinal adhesive bandages of his."

Chief Noble agreed, "I know for sure where there's one of Ban Daid's adhesive bandages still stuck where he left it—on Otto Philia's front door."

And there it was, still there, just outside the door from a recent crime scene as the chief purported. Rubber-gloved, Daed delicately tugged on the adhesive strip, which was just to the left of a door knocker shaped like cartoon dog bone. "What up, Canine?" said Daed to the deceased Otto Philia and to the adhesive bandage, half sentimentally and half in jest. He pulled the little sore stopgap away from the wooden door's surface and immediately noticed a blood-like stain on the center square of gauze, showed it to the chief.

The chief, beguiled, studied the incarnadine splotch before placing it tidily in a clear plastic evidence bag. "I'll be damned, Oversoul, if that doesn't look like a bloodied bandage to me. We'll get it to the lab and rule out sap and paint and such, see if this substance matches the poison found in your alphabet biscuits."

"Those weren't my alphabet biscuits, Chief," protested Daed as he reflexively operated Otto's dog-bone door knocker three times for emphasis. "How many times do I need to defend myself in these matters, when the queen has already given me her pardon?"

"You're right. They're not necessarily your

biscuits, but they are your recipe, Oversoul. That has been proven by forensics."

"My recipe," stated Daed to himself and he would have stated more to himself and to the chief if the front door of the Philia mansion hadn't just then opened in response to his three, loud, prior knocks.

"Hello, friends. My name is Winnay Le Poux. What can I do for you today?" greeted Winnay Le Poux of American reality television's *Shocking Romantic Partners of Famous People* fame. He was indeed quite shocking to Daed and to the chief in his wide dimensions, his lisp, his overalls with no shirt underneath, and his ungainly and gentle manner and sway in the doorway.

"Who are you and what are you doing standing inside an active crime scene?" inquired the shocked chief.

"I already told you both, I'm Winnay Le Poux, one of the stars of *Shocking Romantic Partners of Famous People*. I'm Hissy Fit's long-term, live-in, lovin' boyfriend and, truth be told, I'm not sure who's more famous and who's more shockin' right now, Hissy Fit or me. Otto Philia is my dear friend and I thought the yellow tape around his house was a *VIP, roped-off, tie a yellow ribbon 'round a tree or pole or somethin' and a 'Welcome, how do you do, Winnay Le Poux?'* kind of thing."

The chief, still shocked, did his best to set Winnay straight, "No, it's a sort of *Back off, Winnay Le Poux, there's been a murder here and no one gives a dingle or a damn who's more famous or shocking than anyone else as long as a bloody murderer is on the loose.*"

"Oh, that's a much different scenario," acknowledged Winnay, "like a reality cop show where the reality television stars on the show help the real cops solve the actual crimes. I can help you with that. Most reality TV shows don't do it right. I can show you how to do it, how to find out who the murderer was who killed Otto. I'm free to do it right now, to show the two of you how to do it."

Shock and now aftershock for both Daed and the chief affected the chief's attempt to decline Winnay's offer, "I... don't... know... what... to... say... to... you, Mr. Le Poux. Oversoul?"

"We... don't... know... what... to... say, Winnay," recapitulated Daed.

Winnay confessed unabashedly, "I get that almost every day of my life, friends. Now what's the name of your show?"

"Lambshire," Daed and the chief answered in unison without hem or haw, both having hoped that a one-word answer might serve as a monolithic adhesive bandage over the oozing wound of Winnay Le Poux's flapping gums."

"Lambshire?" double-checked Winnay.

"Yes!" reinforced policeman and poet policeman.

"But what was that other word you used before?" Winnay wondered loudly. "*Overalls* or *oversoul* or somethin'? *Oversoul*," he recalled and then called out, "That's it! I like that one better. I think that should be the name of your show. You should change the name of your reality television show from *Lambshire* to *Oversoul*." Winnay took a long-awaited breath and smiled proudly at his titular conclusion. "I told you I'd show you how to do it. That's how you do it."

Daed and Chief Noble exchanged looks of less shock now than marvel at this immense, unkempt, stultiloquent man in the murder scene threshold, this grotesque possible key to understanding not only what happened to Otto Philia, Zoe and Lord Frisbee Word, but what on earth had become of humanity.

NEVERENDING KNOT

by Jodie Dalgleish

Needlelace, needlepoint, 'points in air' are spun to the end of our lace
mesh dress, as the stitches of all the small spoken bones in the mouth
take a turn of where she's pulling your mouth's thread to her thread's
mouth, like she has a language, turned by her, by you, to fibres spun in on
the outstretched surface of limbs, spun to a thigh just as a touch follicle turns
to lace on the skin; tongue to trace an oversewn body, lace to trace air's body
in the *ponto in aere*[1] of all the small spoken bones in the mouth, air-pointed
honeycomb of carbonate bones, patterns of an aspirate net of chalked
bones, decorative net of air's, regrettable, bones, of aspirate bones, cut to
lace on the skin; air's crack of small bones like bird's bones, honeycomb
of aspirate honeycomb bones, reticulate small-crack bones of air's lace
spun in to the end of a limb's skin,

like she has a language,

end falling like a touch of lace down your spine, all the small-laced vertebrae
touched to its air's lace brace, an air-pointed honeycomb of mouth's lace,
a mouth's brace of its perforations and picks: net end of its honeycomb,
knot honeycombed to net; trace of a mouth's small breaks spun to a lily's
body, spun to a petaline touch on the skin, on a body like air's lilies, skin's
honeycombed bone of a lily stitch, in an arm, two arms, brace spun in on a thigh,
or a cheek, a white-cheeked brace of wings, in the wheeled turning aspirate bone
flesh of their lily, spun in on the skin, reticulate lily stitch spun to touch on bone-
laced lilies, white lilies of a lilied skin, spun to touch on a limb, end organ of a
skin's bone surface noosed, pricked in the small aspirations of bones like bird's
bones, a bone body's air-strung brace of a lily's body, stitch-strung bone lily's
break, mouth's brace of air's iterate lily, net strung to bone's brace of white
mouthed lilies, break to air's mouthed stitch,

like she has this language,

stitching picks to the air's meshed lace of her body, lilied bones to count
air's boned bodies, oversewn cite of air's honeycombed bones, on the skin,
looped to tally air's lace of the small lilied bones of our bodies, reticulate net
to spin bone breaks to the air's skin body, bone length lace of a text, to turn
an arm's length of the skin's boned body to the air's turning bones spun of
white stitched lilies: How do you sound the turn of small bones aspirately
cracking, repeatedly, in the air a mouth nets? [Put your hand in front of your
lips and hear the mouth's 'Crack' of air's plosives on your skin.] Where do we
stitch lace to the bones' break of our texts? [Reach a limb to the lip of the lily of

---

1 Needlelace, needlepoint, or *'ponto in aere'* became the practice of stitching 'the slenderest circumlocutions of threads in
a kind of architecture with no foundations, floating in the air [over paper], almost intangibly, with knots and nets': *Burano:
The Lace Museum.*

a mouth turning small broken bones to the spin of its laced thread?] Her laced
bones', your bones', mouth, spinning lilies as if bones aerate the picked end
of wings stitched to a document, dress of our aspirate body, in its air.

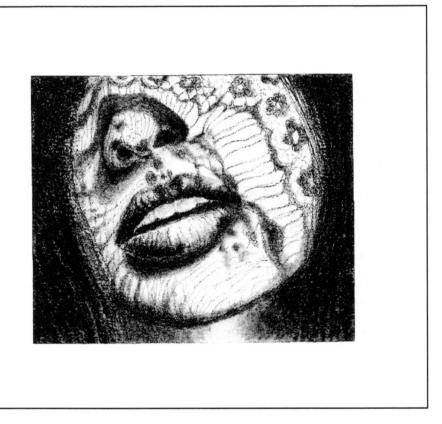

CONTRIBUTORS

D. S. BUTTERWORTH

D. S. Butterworth teaches literature and creative writing at Gonzaga University in Spokane, Washington. Algonquin Books published his creative non-fiction book, *Waiting for Rain: A Farmer's Story*. Lost Horse Press published his books of poems, *The Radium Watch Dial Painters* and *The Clouds of Lucca*. His new book, *drunken man on a bicycle*, is published by Lynx House & University of Washington Press.

NATHANIEL CALHOUN

Nathaniel Calhoun lives in the Far North of Aotearoa New Zealand. He works with teams that monitor, protect and restore biodiversity in ecosystems around the world. He has published or upcoming work in *Guest House, takahē, DMQ, Misfit, Quadrant & Landfall*. Quite rarely he tweets @calhounpoems.

LAYLAGE COURIE

Laylage Courie is a writer and maker of strange things from words. Those things include collage, audio recordings, poems, plays, unclassifiable work, and the art-pop concept album *these fountains rare here* which is available everywhere you download and stream music. Her work has appeared in *Fence, The Exposition Review, Adbusters, Permafrost, Wild Roof*, in *international performance journals*, and on stages all over downtown NY. Join her at luminouswork.org or follow @laylage on Instagram.

JODIE DALGLEISH

Jodie Dalgleish is a writer, curator and sound artist living in Luxembourg. After ten years of creating exhibitions for New Zealand's Art Museums, she is now focused on exploring the possibilities and constraints of language, especially as it explores lived, sensorial, experience. Living in, and traveling between, different countries (NZ; U.S.A; France; Italy; Germany; and Luxembourg), has been germane to her (multilingual) practice. Most recently, her poems have been published in *Landfall* (NZ); *Shearsman Magazine* and T*he Long Poem Magazine* (UK); *Salzburg Poetry Review* (Austria); and *Les Cahiers Luxembourgeois*.

ELIE DOUBLEDAY

Elie Doubleday attended Hamilton College, where she majored in Creative Writing and Hispanic Studies. Born and raised in Portland, Oregon, she is a west-coaster at heart, though she's moved to Boston for work. You'll be hard pressed to catch her without her dog, Wilhelmina Mae. Her poems have previously appeared in the *VoiceCatcher Journal, the Topic Journal,* and *Cordelia Press*. You can find her at @elo2day on Instagram.

KEVIN GRIFFITH

Kevin Griffith has published in numerous journals and is a four-time recipient of the Individual Artist Grant in Poetry from the Ohio Arts Council. He teaches at Capital University in Columbus, Ohio.

HAJAR HUSSAINI

Hajar Hussaini in an Afghan Poet. She received her MFA from the Iowa Writers' Workshop. She currently teaches an asynchronous poetry writing course, and works on the English translation of a Farsi novel. Her first book of poems is forthcoming from the University of Iowa Press in Fall 2022. Her works have appeared in *Pamenar, Atlanta Review, Pocket Samovar,* and elsewhere.

RICHARD KOSTELANETZ

Individual entries on Richard Kostelanetz's work in several fields appear in various editions of *Postmodern Fiction, Contemporary Poets, Contemporary Novelists, Who's Who in American Art, Directory of American Scholars, Advocates for Self-Government, The Facts on File Companion to American Poetry, Merriam-Webster's Dictionary of American Writers, Contemporary Jewish-American Dramatists and Poets, Baker's Biographical Dictionary of Musicians, The HarperCollins Reader's Encyclopedia of American Literature,* and *The Greenwood Encyclopedia of Multiethnic American Literature.*

MARC LERNER

Marc Lerner is a writer living in Sydney, Australia. His work has also been published in *Typishly.*

P. S. LUTZ

P. S. Lutz is a romantic iconoclast who possesses ancient and progressive literary sensibility. Five of his mythic operas have been produced on New York City stages since 2015.

KIRK MARSHALL

Kirk Marshall (@AttackRetweet) is a Brisbane-born writer, teacher, and fundraising specialist living in Melbourne, Australia. He has written for more than eighty publications, both in Australia and overseas, including *Vol. 1 Brooklyn* (U.S.A.), *Word Riot* (U.S.A.), *3:AM* Magazine (France), *Le Zaporogue* (France/Denmark), *(Short) Fiction Collective* (U.S.A.), *The Vein* (U.S.A.), *Danse Macabre* (U.S.A.), *WHOLE BEAST RAG* (U.S.A.), *Gone Lawn* (U.S.A.), *The Seahorse Rodeo Folk Review* (U.S.A.), *The Journal of Unlikely Entomology* (U.S.A.) and *Kizuna: Fiction for Japan* (Japan). He was editor of *Red Leaves*, the English-language / Japanese bi-lingual literary journal. *Feverglades*, a swamp gothic literary thriller, is his first novel.

FRANK MEOLA

Frank Meola has published work in a variety of forms and places, including *New England Review* and the *New York Times*. He frequently writes on American culture and history, most recently an essay on the complexities of Hispanic identity in America (based partly on his own experience). Several of his short stories have won or been finalists in fiction contests. His novel *Clay* was published in summer 2021, and he is at work on a new novel that juxtaposes the present and the 19th century. He has an MFA from Columbia and a PhD from UCLA and teaches writing at NYU. He lives in Brooklyn, NY with his husband and their two cats.

ABBY MINOR

Abby Minor lives in the ridges and valleys of central Pennsylvania, where she works on poems, essays, quilts, and projects exploring reproductive politics. Her first book is *As I Said: A Dissent* (Ricochet Editions, 2022).

LAUREL MIRAM

Laurel Miram is a Detroit-born storyteller and essayist. Her work appears in *SmokeLong Quarterly, OPEN: Journal of Arts & Letters*, the *Eastern Iowa Review*, and elsewhere. She is a senior editor with *The Lascaux Review*.

M. ANN REED

M. Ann Reed teaches the Organic Unity Study of Literature in support of the Deep Ecology Movement for global and local students. Awarded a doctorate in Theater Arts/Performance Studies that included World Literature, she resonates with theater's and literature's dynamic complimentarity, which she taught in Traditional Cultures that regard such creative works medical arts. *Antithesis Literary Arts Journal* of University of Melbourne, *Azure: A Journal of Literary Thought, Burningword, Eastern Iowa Review, Parabola, Proverse, Hong Kong*, and *Psychological Perspectives* are homes for her poems. Finishing Line Press published her chapbook, making oxygen, remaining inside this pure hollow note.

JESSE SCHOTTER

Jesse Schotter teaches English at Ohio State University and is the author of *Hieroglyphic Modernisms*. His essays have been published by *Full Stop* and *Electric Lit*.

LELAND SEESE

Leland Seese's poems appear or are forthcoming in *RHINO, The Chestnut Review, Rust + Moth, The Stonecoast Review*, and many other journals. His debut chapbook, *Wherever This All Ends*, was released in 2020 by Kelsay Books. He and his wife live in Seattle, where they are foster-adoptive parents of six.

GREG SENDI

Greg Sendi is a Chicago writer and former fiction editor at *Chicago Review*. His career has included broadcast and business journalism as well as poetry and fiction. In the past two years, his work has appeared or been accepted for publication in a number of literary magazines and online outlets, including *Apricity, Beyond Words Literary Magazine, The Briar Cliff Review, Burningword Literary Journal, Clarion, Coffin Bell, CONSEQUENCE, Eclectica, Flashes of Brilliance, Great Lakes Review, The Headlight Review, Kestrel, The Masters Review, New American Legends, Plume, Pulp Literature, San Antonio Review, Sparks of Calliope, Third Wednesday* and *upstreet*.

JULIE STIELSTRA

Julie Stielstra lives in the Chicago suburbs, but escapes regularly to central Kansas. Her short fiction has been published in *Zahir Tales, Potomac Review, Bellevue Literary Review, New Plains Review, The Examined Life Journal, Wordrunner eChapbooks*, and *Zizzle Lit*. Minerva Rising Press named her historical novella Pilgrim the winner of their 2016 novella contest, and her 2020 novel *Opulence, Kansas* received gold medal awards for young adult fiction from the Midwest Independent Publishers Association and the High Plains Books Awards. She blogs on books, writing, reading, animals and whatever else takes her fancy at juliestielstra.com.

SARAMANDA SWIGART

Saramanda Swigart has a BA in postcolonial literature and an MFA in writing and literary translation
from Columbia University. Her short work, essays,
and poetry have appeared in *Oxford Magazine, Super-
stition Review, The Alembic, Fogged Clarity, Ghost Town,
The Saranac Review,* and *Euphony* to name a few. She
has been teaching literature, creative writing, and
argumentative writing and critical thinking at City
College of San Francisco since 2014.

VERONICA TANG

Veronica Tang is a senior at Harvard University,
studying Computer Science and English. She adores
differential privacy, cryptography, and mythology.
She is also the co-founder of All Girls STEM Society. When she isn't cranking out problem sets for her
engineering classes, she can be found scribbling in
notebooks by a window in Widener Library.

AZURE: A Journal of Literary Thought
www.LazuliLiteraryGroup.com

NOTES